Lucky raced toward the valley, leaping over fallen branches and scattering leaves. He should have trusted his instincts. Deep down he'd *known* that he was not supposed to leave the Pack. But he had trotted away like a Lone Dog, and now his friends were vulnerable.

Who will protect them if I don't?

SURVIVORS

Also by ERIN HUNTER

WARRIORS

THE NEW PROPHECY

POWER OF THREE

SURVIVORS

A HIDDEN ENEMY

ERIN HUNTER

HARPER
An Imprint of HarperCollinsPublishers

With special thanks to Gillian Philip

For Jamie Philip

A Hidden Enemy

Copyright © 2013 by Working Partners Limited

Series created by Working Partners Limited

Endpaper art © 2012 by Frank Riccio

For information address HarperCollins Children's Books,
a division of HarperCollins Publishers,
10 East 53rd Street, New York, NY 10022.
www.harpercollinschildrens.com

Library of Congress Cataloging-in-Publication Data

Hunter, Erin.

    A hidden enemy / Erin Hunter.—First edition.

        pages cm.— (Survivors ; #2)

Summary: "Lucky and the rest of the Leashed Dogs have settled in the
forest—but a vicious Pack has claimed the land, and will stop at nothing to
ensure that it is theirs alone"—Provided by publisher.

    ISBN 978-0-06-210262-1 (pbk.)

    [1. Dogs—Fiction. 2. Wild dogs—Fiction. 3. Survival—Fic-
tion. 4. Adventure and adventurers—Fiction. 5. Forests and
forestry—Fiction. 6. Fantasy.] I. Title.

PS7.H916625Hid 2013   2013007301

[Fic]—dc23   CIP

                                                            AC

Typography based on a design by Hilary Zarycky

14 15 16 17 18 OPM 10 9 8 7 6 5 4 3 2 1

❖

First paperback edition, 2014

PACK LIST

LONE DOGS

LUCKY—gold-and-white thick-furred male

OLD HUNTER—big and stocky male with a blunt muzzle

LEASHED DOGS

BELLA—gold-and-white thick-furred female, Lucky's littermate (sheltie-retriever mix)

DAISY—small white-furred female with a brown tail (Westie/Jack Russell mix)

MICKEY—sleek black-and-white Farm Dog (Border Collie)

MARTHA—giant thick-furred black female with a broad head (Newfoundland)

BRUNO—large thick-furred brown male Fight Dog with a hard face (German Shepherd/Chow mix)

SUNSHINE—small female with long white fur (Maltese)

ALFIE—small and stocky blunt-faced dog with mottled brown-and-white fur

WILD PACK (IN ORDER OF RANK)

ALPHA:

huge half wolf with gray-and-white fur and yellow eyes

BETA:

small swift-dog with short gray fur (also known as Sweet)

HUNTERS:

FIERY—massive brown male with long ears and shaggy fur

SNAP—small female with tan-and-white fur

MULCH—black long-haired male with long ears

SPRING—tan female hunt-dog with black patches

PATROL DOGS:

MOON—black-and-white female Farm Dog (mother to Squirm, a male black-and-white pup; Nose, a female black pup; and Fuzz, a male black-and-white pup)

DART—lean brown-and-white female chase-dog

TWITCH—tan chase-dog with black patches and a lame foot

OMEGA:

small, black, oddly-shaped dog with tiny ears and a wrinkled face (also known as Whine)

PROLOGUE

Yap pawed excitedly after a shiny green beetle. *You won't defeat me, bug!* he thought. There was nowhere for his prey to hide now. He was Yap the Hunter, Yap the Swift, Yap the Brave! Fierce warrior of Lightning and the Sky-Dogs!

I'm coming for you. . . .

He was pawing at the wriggling critter, using his best scary barks to let the bug know it was doomed, when he heard an eerie howl. Fur prickled on the back of Yap's neck, and he cocked his head, a shiver running through him.

A dog? Is it another dog?

The beetle had vanished under the white fence, but Yap no longer cared. Getting away from the yard-boundary had suddenly become much more important than hunting. Tumbling back clumsily, he bounded across the grass and into the shed, where the warmth and smells were comforting and familiar. His littermates greeted his return with a wild chorus of yipping, and he squeezed in among them beneath his mother's belly.

At last their nuzzling and licking calmed his thumping heart, and he felt his courage creeping back.

"What was that noise?" he whimpered. "Did you hear it? Did you?"

"Yes! Yes!"

"We heard it!"

"A scary dog!"

"Now, now, little ones." Mother-Dog licked their faces fondly. "That wasn't a dog. That was a wolf, and he won't come here."

Wolf. The word sent a new tremor of fear through Yap's body, and he felt the same nervous prickling in the skin of his brothers and sisters. It did not sound like a nice word. It sounded like a word to be afraid of. . . .

There was amusement in Mother-Dog's soft voice as she continued. "There's no need to worry. Wolves are not so very different from us, you know. They have four legs, and fur, and teeth. They're fast and strong and fierce, but they're wild and cunning and crafty too."

"I bet I could outsmart a wolf!" announced Squeak.

"I certainly hope not!" said Mother-Dog. "That's not how dogs should behave. Dogs are clever, but we're not devious.

We are noble and honorable. You pups must always remember that."

"When it howled," said Snip timidly, "it sounded a bit like a dog."

"Wolves and dogs are connected, Snip, and that connection goes back a long, long time. But that does not mean they are to be trusted. If you ever see a wolf, keep your distance. Run away if you have to."

"Why?" asked Yap, his head cocked in confusion.

"Because a wolf will sink his teeth into your flesh the moment your back is turned. Never get close to a wolf. Nuzzle did, and she regretted it. Don't you remember the story? Nuzzle was always much too curious for her own good. She followed the wolves when she heard them howling, because she was brave as well as inquisitive."

"I'm brave too!" interrupted Squeak.

"There's brave and there's foolish, Squeak! The Wild Wolf-Pack caught and trapped Nuzzle beneath the First Pine, and their leader, Greatfang, would have killed her for spying on them.

"But Nuzzle was Lightning's grandpup, and even though Lightning had gone to live with the Sky-Dogs by then, he still watched over his kin. When he saw Nuzzle in danger, he leaped

3

to earth and set fire to the First Pine and Greatfang both! The Wild Wolf-Pack fled in terror, and that's the only reason Nuzzle grew up to be the fierce Warrior-Dog Wildfire. The rest of us cannot rely on Lightning to come and save us, so we must learn from Nuzzle's mistakes."

Distantly the howling echoed again, and the pups cuddled even closer together as their Mother-Dog pricked her ears to listen. Yap felt himself relax. Mother-Dog's flank was so warm, and her heart beat a comforting *thump-thump* against his ear. She would protect them all.

Yap squirmed closer beneath her foreleg. "Even if the wolf came, we'd be all right, wouldn't we?"

Squeak gave a scornful yip.

"Don't be silly, Yap!" she said. "You heard what Mother said— the wolf can't get us here!"

"You're right." Amusement rumbled in the Mother-Dog's throat. "The wolf would never come here. You're all safe, so it's time you went to sleep."

Yap tucked his nose under his paw, cozy and comforted, but he couldn't help twitching an ear at the chilling wail of the wolf as it faded into the distance. *I'm going to be smart,* he thought. *Not*

like Nuzzle. I'm going to stay away from wolves.

Safe and warm, nestled in the Pup Pack: This was how life should be. Far from the Wild, and far from wolves, in the protective huddle of his family. . . .

CHAPTER ONE

"Our territory! Ours!"

Birds took off with an alarmed clatter and screech from the treetops, and disturbed leaves fluttered down around Lucky's paws.

He stood stiff and trembling, gazing back the way he'd come. That was his Pack in the valley—no, not his Pack, but his *friends*. And those ferocious barks told him one thing: They were in terrible danger.

Terrible danger he was not there to help them fight.

Lucky glanced around, torn. Since just after sunup, when he'd left his friends to fend for themselves, he had traveled a long way. He could make out the misty silhouette of the far hills in the distance, and now that he was a good way from the valley he was able to look down on almost the entire forest. Indeed, he'd nearly climbed clear of the trees, and close in front of him was the ridge he'd been heading for. The sight of it had been spurring him on, making his legs run faster and faster—but now he stood as still as a tree.

His friends needed him.

Heart pounding, Lucky bolted back the way he'd come.

Forest-Dog! Don't let them come to any harm! Let me get there in time. . . .

He raced toward the valley, leaping over fallen branches and scattering leaves. He should have trusted his instincts. Deep down he'd *known* that he was not supposed to leave the Pack. But he had trotted away like a Lone Dog, and now his friends were vulnerable.

Who will protect them if I don't?

He could still hear the howls of anger, dog voices that he didn't recognize mingled with the barks of his litter-sister and the rest of the Leashed Dogs.

"Our land, our water! Get out!"

"Everyone together! Stay with me!"

Lucky's powerful hind legs brought him quickly to the crest of a small hill and he scrabbled to a halt before his momentum could take him plunging down.

Wait, Lucky . . . find out the lay of the land before you dash into trouble.

Lucky's keen gaze searched the valley below. It opened out into broad and lush meadows beyond the thick woods. It had seemed ideal for the Leashed Dogs. There were places for Mickey to hunt and for Martha to swim, plenty of shelter for Sunshine and Alfie and Daisy, wide ranges for Bruno and Bella to explore. He should have known that other dogs would have had the same idea. Of course another Pack had gotten to the valley before them, and now those dogs were defending their territory.

In the distance, silver light glinted on a smooth expanse of water; farther off and next to the forest's edge ran the river where he'd last seen the Leashed Dogs. Lucky bounded down the hill, heading toward it.

The hostile Pack's growls and barks made Lucky's fur prickle with anger and fear. But he knew if he burst out from the forest in broad daylight he'd be seen at once, so he made himself go carefully.

Something had changed about the river since he'd left his friends there. *A strangeness,* Lucky thought. And then he remembered the streams and pools close to the destroyed city. They had the same scent of danger that Lucky was picking up now.

Horrified, Lucky stopped and stared. There was a nasty green slick on the surface of the water. This was supposed to be a safe haven! The river was supposed to be clean, *pure*—and it had been, or they'd thought so when they found it yesterday.

But now, Lucky could see the deadly stain spreading down-river.

I led my friends to poisoned water!

Was there no getting away from the taint of death that the Big Growl had brought? At this end of the river, even the trees and bushes at the water's edge looked half-dead, shriveled and broken as if a giant dog had chewed on them. As he ran across the hillside parallel to the stream, Lucky's heart felt heavy in his chest. If the Big Growl's sickness could infect even this place, there might be nowhere else for the dogs to go. Nowhere they could be safe.

"Get out!"

A vicious howl split the air, and Lucky heard the panicked yelping of confused dogs and a sharp yip of pain. He raced along and down the hillside, claws skidding on stone. When he broke out of a line of thick scrub, he caught sight of them at last.

His friends looked small and vulnerable against the attacking Pack: a wild-looking band of large dogs, stiff-legged and snarling. Now and again, one would spring forward to give a brutal volley of barks.

"You've got it coming, Leashed Dogs!"

He could hear Bella's voice, too—quieter, more frightened, but still brave: "It's all right, everyone. Stay together. Sunshine, get behind Bruno. Martha, help Daisy."

Skulking low to the ground, crouching in the shadow of a huge boulder, Lucky counted seven dogs in the enemy Pack. Blood surged through his body and he felt a powerful impulse to race right into the battle, but his instincts, learned on the city streets, held him back. He realized with a rush of relief that the fighting had stopped for the moment. The other Pack was just taunting and insulting Bella's Pack—if Lucky raced in now, the situation could become deadly again. The hostile Pack might decide to finish the smaller dogs quickly so they could concentrate on him.

Right now a couple of huge dogs were lunging and snapping at little Sunshine and Daisy, not biting to kill but making them flinch away in terror.

"Keep them off-balance," some dog said in a low growl. "Spring, watch your side!" One of the Wild Dogs leaped to her right, heading Sunshine off from escape as the small dog scuttled from behind Bruno toward the shelter of some underbrush. Lucky looked around for the dog that had given the orders, but couldn't see him.

Lucky knew that if any of the bigger Leashed Dogs dashed to Sunshine's and Daisy's defense, the rest of the hostile Pack would dart in at their flanks, biting and worrying till the defenders were harried and worn. When it came to the real fight, to claws and teeth and torn skin, Bella and the others would already be exhausted. He'd seen it before, sneaky but efficient, in the brutal bands of dogs he'd tried to avoid in his city days.

He would have to surprise these Wild Dogs, using tactics as cunning and dirty as their own. *Don't just jump in,* he told himself. *Be as wily as the Forest Dog.*

In the shadows, Lucky could get much closer before he pounced, so long as he kept downwind. He dodged through the trees, and as he crept from behind a ridge he caught his first sight of the hostile Pack's leader.

Their Alpha dog.

Huge and gray-furred, he looked lithe and graceful, yet powerful, too. He wasn't joining the battle, but kept giving his Pack sharp orders.

"Keep at their heels! Teach them nobody invades our territory!" He threw his head back and let out a long, snarling howl.

Lucky felt prickles of fear in his fur, his stomach clenching with foreboding as he crept forward.

That's no dog. . . .

No wonder the strange Pack's tactics were as cunning as a wolf's. Lucky had never seen one of those distant dog-cousins close up, but from vague glimpses and half-remembered tales he recognized the pale eyes, savage teeth, and shaggy fur. And there was no mistaking that vicious howl; Lucky had heard something like it once, a long time ago. A memory rippled through his body— a memory not of something seen, but something *heard*.

This powerful gray dog must be half wolf! Lucky had heard of such dogs, but had never met one.

There were another two dogs keeping their eyes trained on the larger Leashed Dogs, though they occasionally looked to their leader and whined for his instructions. Lucky guessed they were directly below the dog-wolf in the strict Wild Pack hierarchy. One was a huge dark-furred dog with a brutally strong neck and mighty jaws. He was watching Martha carefully, but though she was the biggest of the Leashed Dogs, Lucky could see she was already limping on one leg, leaving bloody paw prints when she tried to get out of his way.

The other Wild Dog was a far thinner swift-dog who dodged and circled the fight, moving so fast Lucky's eyes could barely follow her, snapping out orders with a brisk efficiency. She was smaller than the dark-furred dog and fragile-looking, but she seemed very much in command of her underlings.

Maybe it was only her shape and coloring, but Lucky couldn't help being painfully reminded of Sweet, who had escaped with him from the Trap House when all their fellow captive dogs had died.

But this dog didn't have Sweet's good temper. Whoever she was, she would make crow's meat of the Leashed Dogs if her Alpha gave the order to charge.

Forest-Dog, I need all your skill and cunning. . . .

Lucky stalked forward, muscles bunched and tense, still careful to stay safely downwind. He was within a few dog-lengths of the fight now, and they hadn't scented him yet. If he could give them enough of a shock, the Leashed Dogs might have time to get away—yes, just a swift run and a sudden spring . . .

Then he froze again, one paw raised. Not five long-strides away, a small deep-chested dog had hurtled through the scuffle. Lucky's breath stopped in his throat.

Alfie!

The young Leashed Dog skidded to a halt right in front of the huge Alpha. His trembling hindquarters betrayed his fear, but his hackles were up and his lips were drawn back in a defiant snarl. The dog-wolf stared at Alfie, his head cocked as the smaller dog unleashed a volley of furious barks.

"You let us go! Let my friends go! Who says this is your land?"

13

For a moment, the Alpha seemed to waver between contempt and amusement.

Alfie continued his brave barking, his head whipping from side to side, as though he hoped the extra movement would make him look bigger, more threatening. "We're only looking for clean water—you attacked us! You're bad dogs!" Then his gaze fell between the straggly trees, and his eyes met Lucky's. Alfie seemed to swell to twice his size with happiness, renewed courage making his barks louder and more threatening. Lucky could almost hear the thoughts racing through the smaller dog's head.

Lucky's back. . . . Now we'll be fine. . . . We'll win this fight!

Lucky felt a fierce trembling in his flanks as he realized that he had given Alfie the courage to believe that he could stand up to the dog-wolf.

Alfie wrinkled his muzzle, baring his teeth at his massive enemy.

No!

Lucky's muscles bunched to spring forward, but it was too late. Alfie had flung himself at the huge dog-wolf. The Alpha barely moved. A single swipe of one massive paw slammed the brave Leashed Dog to the ground. Alfie rolled over once, and stopped, lying stunned and still. Blood spilled from a massive tear in his side.

Lucky stumbled to a halt. He wanted to howl with rage and anguish. If his friend hadn't seen him, he surely would never have had the nerve to charge at the half wolf.

Why did you have to see me, Alfie? Why—

Lucky's fur and skin prickled as the ground started shaking beneath his paws. It was as though the Earth-Dog shared Lucky's anger.

Then—*wham!*—Lucky was thrown forward, stumbling as the whole world shook again. He hit the ground and tumbled, but managed to jump back onto all four paws, his entire body trembling.

Another Big Growl!?

The fighting stopped as every dog crouched low, steadying himself. The Wild Pack all looked to their Alpha, who braced his legs against the trembling earth for a second before letting out a chilling howl.

"It's happening again! Pack, to me!"

A tree right beside Lucky creaked and groaned and started to fall. Lucky scrambled out of its path just before it slammed into the solid rock of the hillside and started rolling across the ground that was splitting apart at Lucky's paws. Soon, the air was filled with the shrieks of tortured wood as more and more trees fell, hitting the rocks with crashes that sounded like thunder.

Lucky fled in a panic, not knowing or caring what direction he was taking.

All that mattered was getting away from the Growl.

But the Growl was everywhere, above and around him. The whole earth seemed to slide treacherously beneath his paws. *No, not again! Don't let the Growl ruin this place too. . . .*

As he bolted, Lucky glanced back to see that the other dogs, both Wild and Leashed, were also fleeing in blind terror. The shuddering earth split, a wound tearing itself down the center of the valley. A bundle of pale fur was a blur at the edge of his vision. Someone was falling into the crack. Lucky snapped his head away and veered to the right, afraid to see the death of any dog. He spotted Mickey and Bruno struggling to drag Alfie's limp form toward shelter, and Martha limping painfully away from the crashing trees.

My Pack!

Instinct spurred him to run after them, but it was too late. Above him another gigantic tree was creaking and cracking, its roots lifting from the dirt as if it were trying to pull itself free.

Lucky leaped off the clod of earth and roots, tumbling awkwardly to the ground, and a jolt of pain went through his foreleg. For a moment, he couldn't move. But when he looked up and saw the great tree swaying, falling back into place, he thought he was safe—until the shifting ground heaved again, and the great tree toppled toward him.

Terror ripped through Lucky's bones as he lay on his side and stared up at the massive shuddering trunk, his brain rattled by the tree's tortured shriek of death.

He rolled onto his paws, trying to crawl away on his belly.

But there was no escape.

Earth-Dog wants me. . . . thought Lucky, as he heard the mighty tree falling. *I'm not going to get away this time.*

CHAPTER TWO

The tree was coming straight down on him. He heard the creaking roar, felt the rush of wind—

Then Lucky glimpsed the sharp blade of a rocky overhang. With a last surge of desperate energy he scrabbled and slid down a boulder, shooting under the jutting rock. He cowered in its shelter, trembling like a pup under its mother's belly.

For a long moment, all he could hear was the rumbling thunder of the tree crashing down onto the rocks, branches splitting and cracking as they hit the overhang, twigs and shards of bark exploding around him. He flinched as a splinter of wood struck his flank, but he knew he had to keep still. He could not jump up and run, no matter how strong the urge.

Please, Earth-Dog, he thought. *Be merciful.*

Slowly the deafening racket of the tree's collapse rebounded and echoed and faded. All that was left was a blizzard of pine needles. At last, the ground underneath him grew still.

Earth-Dog had stopped growling.

Still trembling, Lucky crept out from his shelter, forcing his body through the thick branches and foliage of the dead tree. Its trunk was as broad as a loudcage, and shudders of horror went through his spine at the thought of how close it had come to falling right on top of him. *I'd be dead now. . . . My body would already be with the Earth-Dog.*

Lucky licked at his leg, but the twinge of pain had faded. He realized with a rush of relief that he wasn't hurt. He'd only just recovered from the slash on his paw from the last Big Growl. It wouldn't do to find himself with another leg wound.

The hillside around him was torn and devastated, as if a giant dog had scraped great gashes in it with its forepaws. Awed, Lucky crept carefully down the uneven slope, hardly daring to pick up his pace. But the area where the dogs had fought was not far below him now, and Lucky trotted more urgently when he reached level ground.

The air was a chaos of scents—damp, wounded earth, roots, blood, and splintered wood. Strongest of all was the smell of dog-fear, though the others had run away from the battle site now. Lucky's ears pricked as he glanced around, hoping he'd see one of his own Pack searching for him. He had no idea where they were now. Had any of the others seen him?

Or just poor Alfie?

As the image of the little dog, broken and wounded, came into his mind, Lucky heard a terrible keening noise. It was the sound of a dog in distress, hurt and helpless.

Lucky glanced around nervously, his fur bristling. Where was the noise coming from? It seemed close, but there was no sign of the dog who was making it.

As he turned, searching, he caught sight of the crack in the earth. Cold horror surged through his body as he remembered the blur of pale fur that he'd seen fall into the split in the ground.

Earth-Dog! he thought. She must have swallowed one of the dogs, showing them her fury at their fighting. Stiff-legged and shivering, Lucky began to back away from the chasm. If Earth-Dog was as angry as that with the battling dogs, who knew what she might do next, or who she might turn her wrath on?

He needed to get as far from the crack in the ground as he possibly could. He didn't know the distressed dog who was making the agonized sound. It wasn't one of the Leashed Dogs—he'd have recognized any of them immediately, even blurred and falling. The pitifully howling dog was a stranger—one of the enemy Pack.

None of that Pack can be trusted. Why should I rescue a stranger?

Still, Lucky's whole coat twitched and tingled. Something was drawing him back, an urge he couldn't resist. He pricked his ears high, straining to hear. Something about that desperate, pleading howl tugged at his recent memory. And the scent . . . it was tantalizingly familiar, but the mess of smells created by the Growl meant that he could not pick it out properly.

Lucky shook himself violently. Of course he couldn't walk away from a dog in danger! It didn't matter if that other dog was friend or foe. Lucky wouldn't be a dog at all if he left one of his own kind to suffer a terrible fate. What had Mother-Dog once said? Noble and honorable. He couldn't betray his own dog-spirit.

Taking a deep breath, Lucky loped carefully to the edge of the chasm. It was very dark but, as his eyes adjusted to the dimness after the bright sunlight, he made out the shape of a cowering creature.

The swift-dog.

It was one of the dog-wolf's lieutenants, the one who had darted back and forth and barked the orders to attack. Now she crouched on a narrow ledge of rock, quivering in fear. Her muzzle lay over the ledge as she stared down, wide-eyed, at the deadly drop; but as Lucky's claws scraped the loose rock on the edge of the crack, shards of stone skittered into the depths, and the swiftdog lifted her head. She stared up at him, petrified.

Lucky took a backward step in surprise.

Sweet!

His friend-behind-the-wire . . . his fellow survivor of the Trap House . . .

When she'd left him alone, in search of Pack companions, he'd wondered if she would be able to survive.

She had—and she was with the Wild Pack!

She was whimpering now, blinking her big eyes against the strong sunlight from above. As she made him out, she gave a sharp whine of shock.

"What are you doing here?"

They both asked the question together, and for a long moment gaped at each other. Then Lucky shook himself.

"Never mind that now, Sweet. You have to get out of there."

She crouched against the rock wall, trembling. "I don't know how."

Lucky took another hesitant step forward, bringing him to the edge of the chasm. He began to crouch, but loose stones slithered beneath his paws and a rain of tiny rocks clattered and pattered into the darkness. *Back!* Lucky stepped hastily away from the drop, his fur lifting.

"You're not far down. Can't you hook your claws over the edge, pull yourself up?"

"I don't think so," she whined. "If I start to climb and lose my grip, I'll—"

"I'll help you. You have to try!"

Slowly, cautiously, Sweet got to her feet and turned in a tight circle, as if she were preparing for sleep. Her tail was tucked tightly between her legs, and her sleek coat seemed to tremble with fear. Hesitantly she rose up on her hind legs and caught the edge with her claws.

"Now kick with your hind legs. And pull! You'll be fine, Sweet—just pull—"

Gradually Sweet hauled herself up the sheer rock, hindpaws flailing. With a whine of terror she started to slip, but Lucky leaned into the crack to seize the scruff of her neck with his teeth, praying to the Earth-Dog that the crumbling stone would hold him. He could no longer encourage Sweet with his barks; he could only drag her upward, feeling her wriggle and thrash in his jaws.

Behind him, he heard a sound he recognized all too well. A violent, ominous creaking. With a desperate growl, Lucky scuffed backward, tugging Sweet hard as the swift-dog gave a final powerful kick with her hind legs. She was up and over the edge, and Lucky shouldered her sideways just as a wounded tree groaned and toppled, slamming into the ground with a crash.

They stood, panting with exhaustion and relief. Lucky blinked and gasped until he got his breath back, his heart hammering away at his belly.

Then they both yelped with joy, colliding as they sprang forward, tumbling over each other, licking and nosing and barking with delight.

"That's the second Big Growl we've outwitted!" said Lucky.

"Yes! Oh, Lucky, you are lucky!" Sweet barked.

"I didn't think I'd see you again!"

"I didn't think I'd see you, Packless Dog!" She nibbled his neck fur happily.

"Sweet . . . " Lucky drew away slightly, remembering the moment he'd laid eyes on her again—when he hadn't even recognized such a fierce, feral dog. "Why was your Pack attacking . . . those dogs?"

Sweet gave a yelp of derision. "Those what? They're barely dogs at all. Did you get a good look at them? How dare those disorganized mutts think of invading our territory?"

"That's—sort of what I mean." Lucky averted his eyes, licking his chops. "They didn't know how to fight, I could tell. Your Pack was"—*cruelly efficient,* he wanted to say—"harsh to them."

Lucky bit back a whine as he wondered why he'd pretended not to know his friends.

Am I ashamed of them?

"Leashed Dogs," snarled Sweet. "I don't know what they were doing here, but they certainly won't be invading real dogs' territory again. They'll know better than that now."

I used to worry about her, he remembered. *I worried that she wouldn't be tough enough to survive. Can this really be the same swift-dog who panicked at the sight of a dead longpaw?*

Catching Lucky's shocked expression, Sweet jabbed her head forward insistently. "It was a necessary lesson. The Leashed Dogs won't make that mistake again. That's best for them as well as us."

"I suppose you're right," Lucky whined, feeling a flash of guilt burn in his belly. *This was my fault.*

"Of course I'm right," said Sweet. "And I was right to go seek out a Pack! I have missed you, Lucky . . . but I found just the Pack I was looking for. They're strong, organized—" She stopped, cocking her head and giving him a quizzical look. "But what brings *you* so far out of the city? I thought you were determined not to leave."

"I couldn't stay," he told her. "There was too much danger . . . you were right about that."

Sweet gave him a playful nudge with her nose. "I'm right about most things."

He licked her jaw affectionately. "I left the city with a Pack"— he wasn't about to mention *which* Pack—"and I was just striking out alone again when I heard the sound of fighting." He dipped his head, giving a sad, but sharp, whine. "Dogs fighting each other! When we've all just escaped the Big Growl! It seemed . . . strange. I was curious." He fell silent, deciding he'd said too much already.

Sweet looked astounded. "*You* were with a Pack? But I thought you hated Packs! I thought that's why you wouldn't come with me."

"It wasn't like that, Sweet." He hesitated, wondering how to explain.

She didn't speak for a moment, her gaze focused on the ground between her paws. When she looked up again, her eyes were angry and full of hurt. "You said you were a 'Lone Dog,' that you wanted to be free and by yourself!"

Lucky felt prickles of regret as he remembered the things he had told her in the Food House, the day he had refused to travel with her.

"I'm not with a Pack," he said. "Not *really*. It just happened. Almost by accident. They didn't know how to get by, so I tagged along. They were strangers, but they needed my help, so I gave it to them. Just like I would have helped *you*, if you hadn't run off and left me behind like you did."

"I didn't want to leave you behind," said Sweet, her voice small. "But you wanted to stay in the city. And I *needed* a Pack. I wish I could make you understand, Lucky."

Inwardly he squirmed. He understood far better than she thought he did. "And you found one. You must have done well, Sweet. They were treating you like a leader during the fight."

"I've advanced quickly," Sweet agreed a little reluctantly. "It's the way of a Pack, that's all. Things change."

Lucky raised his head and sniffed the wind, which was rising again after the stillness that had accompanied the Growl. There were distinct smells of life—and death—creeping into the air.

"I have to get going, Sweet."

"Again? But where will you go?"

Lucky was silent as he thought about it. He was desperate to find Bella and the others, to find out what had become of Alfie, but he couldn't tell Sweet that. He had as good as told her that he had nothing to do with the ragtag Pack she had been fighting. He couldn't go back on that now.

Sweet nuzzled him. "Why don't you come with me, Lucky? Come and meet my Pack. You'll like us. You've just saved my life, so they'll like you."

"I don't know . . ."

"Lucky, you can't survive on your own. What if the next Growl catches you, and there's no one to help you like you helped me? And so many of the streams are poisoned! You might not find clean water to drink. You must come with me!"

A shiver went through Lucky's fur, and he gave himself a brisk shake to disguise it. "I'm sorry, Sweet. I'm still a Lone Dog."

"All dogs should stand together at times like these," said Sweet, her nose turning up. "You're strong, you're clever—you should offer all that to a Pack, not keep it for yourself!" Sweet sounded almost angry, but her voice softened. "You'd be happy, Lucky. I promise."

Lucky averted his gaze, feeling the old stubbornness back in his belly. "I'm happier on my own."

Sweet dipped her head. "I can't make you change your mind, can I? Then I wish you well. Please take care."

"I will." Lucky padded away, still feeling the tug of regret and unable to resist a last look back.

Sweet was already bounding across the broken ground, elegantly leaping over fallen trees. A memory struck him sharply: Sweet bolting from the cold room in the Food House, terrified by the dead longpaw inside, and the destruction of the city outside. Her speed was the same, but in every other way she seemed different. Her head was high and her ears were pricked. Her coat was sleek and the muscles beneath were strong and defined.

Lucky felt the strongest urge to bark after her, to call her back and ask if she'd come with him instead. She'd be a great addition to Bella's Pack. And what if he never saw her again? He was going to miss her. . . .

But it was too late. Sweet was already out of sight, and Lucky would never catch her now. There was nothing left to do but continue his search for the Leashed Dogs.

As he padded on, he felt flutters of fear in his fur. *They'll be all right,* he told himself. *They've survived one Growl already. Surely they'll have survived this one, too. . . .*

CHAPTER THREE

It wasn't difficult to follow the trail of Bella and the others farther into the shattered valley. All Lucky had to do was pad after the trickles and pools of blood that Alfie and Martha had left. The metallic scent of it made his bones and muscles cold; a terrible anxiety drove him on to leap cracks in the ground and force his way through thickets of fallen branches.

At least, he thought, the valley would recover swiftly. Saplings would grow again to replace the trees, and the cracked ground and uprooted bushes would soon be covered with new moss and grass and plants, hiding the damage.

Unlike the city, which would never be able to heal itself.

Leaping on top of a thick pine trunk, Lucky made out the river beyond, very close now. Like the streams near the city, the silver of its surface was tinged with that same iridescent sheen. The poison really had spread this far, even in the short time since he'd left Bella's Pack. Lucky's heart sank. Maybe the valley wouldn't recover as quickly as he'd thought. . . .

There was a ridge of ground that fell sharply toward the river, and tree roots half-exposed by the rush of water jutted out over the bank. When he jumped down it he found a sandy hollow beneath the roots. Huddled there were the seven Leashed Dogs, their hackles stiff with fear.

"You'll be all right," Daisy was saying, licking at Martha's torn leg. "But you shouldn't move around."

Bruno's sturdy body stood over Alfie, who lay still and broken on the ground. Sunshine stared at the little dog, shivering.

"He needs a vet! He really does!" Sunshine whined. "I wish my longpaws were here."

"We all do." Mickey gave her a reassuring lick, but his flanks were trembling.

Then Daisy looked up and caught sight of Lucky. Her eyes widened and she gave a frightened yelp. That set the others off, leaping and scrambling to their feet, falling over one another in their haste. *They must think I'm one of the Wild Dogs,* Lucky realized. He gave a soft reassuring growl, and came out of the deeper shadows so they could see him better.

"It's me," he barked.

Their shock was plain in their faces and their bristling coats, but then Bella's ears pricked and she sprang to meet him, pressing her face to his.

"You came back."

"Lucky!" The others trotted to join her, whining and licking him—all but Bruno, who stayed standing protectively over Alfie. Lucky heard him grumble, "It's a little late for a heroic return, Lucky."

Sunshine and Daisy jumped up to reach his nose, but their old enthusiasm was subdued. Sadness filled the little hollow. Even the acrid scent of the river was overwhelmed by the tang of blood. Hesitantly, Lucky paced forward to where Alfie sprawled, eyes half-closed, panting weakly. His flank rose and fell barely at all.

"Oh, Lucky," whined Mickey. "Is there anything we can do?"

They all fell silent as Lucky nosed Alfie's wound. The skin was split wide and Lucky could see red, glistening muscle like he'd seen on injured prey. The sight of it turned his stomach cold.

A faint whimper came from Alfie's throat, but he couldn't raise his head to greet Lucky. The sand beneath him was stained with thick, dark blood, but it no longer flowed from his side in a strong stream. It had been reduced to a limp trickle that seeped feebly in the slash.

Lucky closed his eyes briefly, hating to have to break such news.

"He isn't bleeding so badly anymore." There was a faint hope in Sunshine's voice that made Lucky's heart turn over.

He licked her muzzle. "Sunshine," he said. "There's nothing we can do for Alfie."

"But . . ." Daisy faltered.

Lucky held her gaze, his heart feeling as heavy as a rock. "There's less blood because the Earth-Dog has taken most of it already. Do you see Alfie's eyes?"

Martha took a hesitant step closer. "They're so blurry—as if he can't see anymore."

"Alfie's essence is flowing out of his body. It's starting to become one with everything else around us." Lucky gazed down at the little dog, his shallow occasional breaths barely lifting his flank.

The Leashed Dogs fell silent again, and Martha lay down to push her nose close to Alfie's. "Oh, my poor little friend."

"This isn't fair!" whimpered Sunshine, raising her pleading eyes to Lucky's. She let out a terrible, mournful howl. "Why did this have to happen?"

Lucky longed to look away, but he knew he couldn't; his friends were grieving. They needed him to be strong.

Bella raised her muzzle and whined, and then Mickey and

Daisy joined in the Pack's howl. Even stolid Bruno gave voice to his misery.

Lucky dipped his head to tenderly lick Alfie's face.

"He was barely more than a puppy," Martha said softly.

Lucky licked each dog's muzzle in turn, trying desperately to give some comfort. "We just won't be able to *see* Alfie, that's all. But he will still be with us, *around* us—in the air and the water and the earth."

Sunshine jerked back from him, and he blinked in surprise.

"What use is that?" she barked. "I liked Alfie being here! In his own body. With us!"

Lucky had no answer. Despite his reassuring words about the spirit essence, he knew just how Sunshine felt. The painful memory struck him again: Alfie, given new heart by Lucky's arrival and desperate to impress him, charging bravely at the dog-wolf and paying with his life.

Oh, Alfie, thought Lucky miserably, *if only I'd stayed out of sight.*

He turned back to the younger dog, bending to lick his nose again very gently. No breath came from Alfie's muzzle now. Bella came to his side, nuzzling Alfie's ear. The others gathered around her.

"I'll miss you, Alfie," mourned Daisy.

"We all will." Mickey nudged his tail gently. "Safe journey, my friend."

"Into the world," added Sunshine, her whines heavy with grief.

Lucky took a small pace backward as he watched them say their farewells. He wished he could *see* Alfie's essence escaping his body. It would be reassuring to watch his spirit flow into the trees, and the air, and the clouds. It would make this so much easier for all of them if they could witness his final journey.

But there was only a lifeless little body lying on the dry earth, and the first faint suggestion of the death-smell. There was nothing inside Alfie's body anymore—no breath, no spirit, no life. Lucky slumped down onto his belly and added his whines of grief to the Pack's.

Sunshine was right: This wasn't fair.

He realized that Sweet had also been right: There was still so much he did not know about Pack life, Pack traditions. There had to be some kind of ceremony, he was sure, but he had no idea what it would be, or how it would go. When a City Dog died, the longpaws came and took him away. Perhaps he should have asked Sweet about that aspect of Pack life. He should have asked her about so many things.

Lucky stood up hesitantly. "I think the best thing—the natural thing—would be to leave Alfie here. Earth-Dog will absorb him when she's ready."

"Leave him?!" cried Sunshine in horror. "I don't want to leave him!"

"Certainly not." Daisy shuddered. "If we do, the crows and the foxes will eat him. We can't do that to Alfie!"

"Daisy's right," Mickey agreed. "When a Leashed Dog died, the longpaws would always bury him—sometimes, they would put flowers and stones on top of the ground, after they put him inside. That's the proper way."

"It's the *longpaw* way," muttered Lucky, but so quietly it was only to himself. The last thing he wanted just now was to upset his friends, who clearly still thought like Leashed Dogs when it came to these sorts of decisions.

"Daisy and Sunshine and Mickey are right." Bella stood squarely on a nearby rock, gazing firmly at them all. She looked like a *real* leader of a Pack. "We should bury him, like his longpaw would have done."

Lucky watched, impressed, as the grief seemed to lift slightly from the Leashed Dog Pack. They nodded to one another, shook out their fur, and stood up straighter. *Yes,* thought Lucky. *It's not about what's normal for Wild Dogs—this is what's right for them.* Alfie wasn't ashamed of having belonged to longpaws. They were doing this for him, so they would do it Alfie's way—the way he would have wanted it.

Besides, at that moment Lucky found himself angry with all the Spirit Dogs.

River-Dog! Forest-Dog! Sky-Dogs! Couldn't you have helped him? Couldn't you have protected our brave friend from that dog-wolf brute?

He was so small. . . .

There was softer earth a little way from the riverbank, and Lucky pitched in to help Bella, Mickey, and Martha make a hole. It didn't take long to dig enough space for Alfie.

Martha was right, Lucky thought, grief burning in his gut. Alfie was barely more than a pup. With all a pup's foolish courage, too. . . .

This would be the best possible place for him. If his spirit was in these trees and this cool earth, deep in the peaceful valley, Alfie would be happy, he decided. And even the river might one day be clean again.

"I wish we had his ball to leave with him," whispered Daisy. "The one he brought . . . the one he brought when—"

"When the longpaw house fell. When he nearly died." Bella's eyes were glimmering with sadness. "We saved him then. Oh,

Sky-Dogs, why couldn't we save him today?"

"We don't have his ball," Bruno growled. "Lucky made us leave the longpaw things behind." He sounded angry, but Lucky could not scent any *real* rage coming from him. The stocky dog was just covering his deep sorrow.

Lucky felt an itch of guilt, but he didn't want to scratch it away. It had been the right thing to do, but now it was feeling wrong. "Earth-Dog will take good care of him," he insisted, but there was a catch in his voice. It sounded like an empty promise, even to his own ears.

Martha picked Alfie up in her jaws, moving slowly and carefully—even though there was no way Alfie would feel pain now. Despite her bad leg, he wasn't much of a burden for her. As she laid his limp body carefully in the hole, the others helped to scrape and kick the earth back over him, until he was hidden from sight for the last time. All the dogs paused and gazed at his final sleeping-place, lit by the dying glow of the sinking sun.

"It feels wrong to leave him," whimpered Daisy.

"I know what you mean," said Lucky. To his surprise, he really did.

"Why don't we stay here, then?" suggested Bella. "Just until the Sun-Dog returns."

"What if those terrible dogs come back?" asked Sunshine as she pawed gently at the mound of soil above Alfie.

Lucky shook his head. "They ran from the Growl, too. I think we should stay with Alfie."

"I like that idea," said Mickey quietly. "We'll guard his body during no-sun. Our way of saying good-bye."

Lucky nodded, an odd heaviness in his throat.

"It feels right," said Sunshine, glancing up at the bigger dogs. "Doesn't it?"

Mickey licked her neck fondly, before scratching at the ground with his claws three times. Then he touched it with his nose. "Earth-Dog," he whined. "Look after our friend." He turned his muzzle to the sky and began to howl.

The sound was eerie and heartrending, and Lucky felt a tremor run through his skin. Then the others began to join in, raising their heads and howling.

"Take care of Alfie, Earth-Dog!"

"Guard him for us!"

"Keep his spirit safe!"

Lucky watched in respectful silence. This was something he had never witnessed, and did not quite understand. Maybe it had never happened before. Maybe it was another way that dogs were changing along with the whole world.

The sky was darkening fast, and Alfie's sad little burial mound was fading into shadow, but still the mournful howling went on. It was the strangest ritual Lucky had ever seen, but he had to admit that it made him feel a little better. He was sure Bella and the others must feel that way too, however sad they were. There was something comforting about passing Alfie formally into Earth-Dog's paws for protection.

Lucky trod his habitual sleep circle, then lay down with his muzzle on his paws. He closed his eyes. The howling was almost soothing. . . .

Abruptly he blinked awake from a half dream, his fur bristling.

In his drifting dream he'd thought it was something else, a sound not of grief but of terrible menace. A memory stirred from long ago. *The howling* . . .

But it was only his friends, still grieving for Alfie.

Lucky closed his eyes again and let sleep wash over him.

CHAPTER FOUR

Lucky could feel the sun on his back. The warmth was comforting after the chill of the night.

Bella walked at his side as they followed the river upstream. Both dogs eyed the water with trepidation; the sinister colors on the surface gave it a strange loveliness in the morning light.

"We should scout around," Bella had said, not long after Lucky had woken up and stretched his back and neck. "See if there's been any sign of those dogs since yesterday."

Lucky sensed that it wasn't just sensible caution on his sister's part. She *needed* to be away from the others for a while.

His litter-sister had something on her mind.

"Tell me what happened when that fight broke out," he suggested at last. "I heard it from far away."

Bella sighed. "It was terrible. But I don't see any way we could have avoided it."

"But how did you cross those dogs? How did it start?"

"Martha was the one who noticed." Bella stopped and wrinkled her muzzle at the stained river. "She came down to swim, and realized straight away that the poisoned water had reached us, and it was still spreading. She ran back to warn us. She was so distressed, but then you know how close Martha feels to the River-Dog."

Lucky growled in agreement. "I noticed the bad water as soon as I saw the river. It's a dark omen, Bella."

"Yes." Bella sighed again. "We knew immediately we couldn't stay. But we thought, it's such a big valley, and so fertile—there *had* to be clean water somewhere close by. So we set off in search of it."

"And you found some?"

"There's a place with a lot of water not far from here. I've never seen so much water in one place—I don't think any of us had. It's strange, Lucky—like the pond at the Dog Park, but so huge, and very still and silent."

"A lake," Lucky said. "So what happened?"

"We were worried about drinking the water, because we'd never seen anything like it. But we were so thirsty. Martha paddled in first, and then Bruno, and suddenly we were all splashing and drinking to our hearts' content. I thought our troubles were over."

"But you'd moved into someone else's territory—"

"Yes." Bella's head and ears drooped. "We didn't even know it until we came across a guard. Just one, and there was a stand-off—he was as shocked as we were, I think. He was a long-legged dog and when he ran away, he was fast. We heard him barking an alarm, and he came back with his whole Pack."

"And they attacked you? Just like that?"

"Not right away." Bella came to a halt, lay down on her belly, and licked disconsolately at a paw. "I tried to reason with them. I asked if we could drink from the lake—if we could at least share that. There was so much water there—more than any dog could ever need!"

Lucky shook his head sadly. "That's not the way it works."

Bella gave an annoyed grumble. "But I couldn't back down, Lucky. I knew my Pack would die if we had to go back and drink from the river. I tried again. I did my best, truly."

"I know you did, Bella." Lucky felt a flash of anger at dogs who could be so unfeeling for anyone who wasn't in their Pack.

Bella's tail thumped the ground, slowly and heavily. "The more I argued, the more I tried to persuade them, the angrier those other dogs got. It was as if they were offended that I would even try. Finally, their leader gave the order to attack, and they went for us. We ran at first, but when we got close to the poisoned river again, we couldn't keep running. . . . "

"And that's where I came in." Lucky licked her nose. "I saw the fight from a long way off, and heard you from even farther. I wanted to help, but I knew I had to be careful. Rushing in could have made things worse. Then Alfie . . ." His voice caught in his throat as he remembered.

If I had been there, if I had been fighting with them, would I have been able to stop all this from happening? Would Alfie still be alive?

Lucky could not help thinking he'd have handled it differently, had it been him in the standoff with the angry dogs. He would never have tried to argue with that dog-wolf once he had refused them. Bella should have backed off humbly, thought of some other strategy—challenging the Wild Pack's Alpha was asking for trouble.

Maybe coming back *had* been a mistake. He knew the others didn't think so, but . . . the Growl had put a stop to the fighting without his help, and perhaps if Lucky hadn't shown his face, Alfie would never have made his stupidly brave attack on the dog-wolf. That guilt still pricked at him.

"Come on," he said at last. "We'd better get back to the others."

Bella rose slowly to her feet, her tail and ears still down, and the two littermates retraced their steps back to the dogs' make-shift camp. All the sunlight and brightness seemed to have been taken out of the day. Lucky almost wished he hadn't asked about the battle.

As soon as they came in sight of the rest of the Pack, Lucky realized how much work there was still to do with these dogs—how desperately they needed a streetwise friend. Mickey was licking so hungrily from an old rain puddle, he was down to the mud at the bottom.

Lucky nudged the older dog away with his nose. "You shouldn't drink that."

Mickey lowered his ears, ashamed. "There isn't any fresh water, Lucky," he said. "Surely this is safer than drinking from that poisoned river?"

Lucky tilted his head thoughtfully. He had to admit, Mickey had a point.

"We can't rely on the rain." He licked his chops uncertainly. "The Earth-Dog drinks it quickly, and what she leaves behind is fouled."

"But Martha's wounded," said Mickey, looking at the big water-dog, who lay washing the bite on her leg with her tongue. "She can't travel far."

"I know!" Daisy leaped up brightly, tail wagging. "Remember we made that offering before, to the Sky-Dogs? Let's do the same for the River-Dog now! If we send him a gift, perhaps he'll clean the water for us!"

The little white dog's head cocked and her tongue lolled. She looked so pleased with her suggestion, Lucky couldn't bear to contradict her. He had never known the Spirit Dogs to intervene as quickly or obviously as that, but who was he to say they wouldn't do so now, in these desperate times? The River-Dog might appreciate an offering, and if there was any dog in the Pack that he might have mercy for, it would be Martha, with her love of water and her big webbed paws.

"Well," he said slowly, "it's worth a try. But what will we give to the River-Dog?"

"Food!" Sunshine barked excitedly. "We'll give him a rabbit—or a squirrel!"

Lucky stared at her, skeptical. "Food? Do you have any to spare?"

Sunshine's ears drooped. "Well . . ."

"No," Bella growled witheringly. "We *don't.*"

"We . . . we could try to find some?" Sunshine suggested, but Lucky could see that even she didn't think it was a good idea.

Daisy gave her a supportive lick on one long-furred ear.

"I think River-Dog would want us to use any food we find to keep ourselves alive. We'll think of something else," she said kindly. Sunshine dipped her head, embarrassed.

Lucky felt a little sorry for Sunshine. If she could suggest, even for a moment, giving their food supplies away so casually, she was still a long way from understanding survival in the Wild.

Mickey was lying with his head on the longpaw glove he'd brought with him all the way from the city, and he suddenly sniffed at it and looked up. "I have an idea. What do we dogs like almost as much as eating?" He glanced around at all of them. "Playing! My longpaw pup would always wear this while he played fetch with me."

"How does that help?" Bella asked.

"All dogs like a game of fetch, don't we? Let's find the River-Dog a really good stick!"

Bella cocked her head, thinking. "That might work."

Lucky wasn't so sure, but Mickey looked enormously pleased with himself. "Come on, then. I bet we can find something *really* special. We'll check with Martha before we offer it, to make sure we find something the River-Dog will like."

Bella gave a bark of approval.

To Lucky it sounded more like Leashed Dog logic—*Why would the River-Dog want anything to play with, as if he needed a longpaw owner to entertain him?*—but if it would make the others feel better, maybe it was worth a try. And perhaps the good intentions behind the gift would win over the River-Dog. Surely he would at least be pleased with the Pack's efforts.

Mickey was already bounding between the remaining trees, sniffing out fallen branches and twigs. The others darted to join him, nosing in the tangled foliage, clearly relieved to have something positive to do. Their excitement was infectious, and Lucky found his hopes rising as he too searched for a fine fetching-stick. It was nice to be moving *toward* something, rather than running *away*.

"How about this one?" grunted Bruno through a mouthful of birch branch.

They all stopped their searching to examine Bruno's find. It was a beautifully shaped stick, smooth and sturdy but bent just enough in the middle to give the best jaw-hold. When they brought it to her, Martha tilted her head, sniffing at the papery silver bark.

"It's beautiful," she announced at last. "I think the River-Dog will like it very much."

They were all yelping and whining with eagerness as they trotted to the riverbank, Martha limping slowly in front carrying the special stick, and Bruno padding beside her, his head proudly held high.

At the crumbling bank, Martha lowered herself onto her forepaws and gently released the gift. The whole Pack helped her nose it into the stream without touching the water. It caught on a tuft of grass but, with a last nudge, it came free and floated off into the deeper water, swirling in the lazy current.

"River-Dog!" whined Martha. "Please help us. We need clean water to drink."

The rest of the Pack yelped in agreement, watching as the stick slid smoothly between rocks and into a fast-flowing channel of white water. It bounced and tumbled in the rushing current, and Sunshine yelped with delight.

"The River-Dog's playing with the stick! See? He really is!"

The dogs panted happily, watching the stick drift downstream into calmer water, creating eddies of rainbow in the filmy green surface. Then it spun out of sight.

Martha's ears drooped. "Poor River-Dog," she said softly. "He must hate that his rivers are poisoned like this. Perhaps he's unwell himself."

"Let's just hope he likes our offering," said Bella, nuzzling her neck. "We've done all we can for now. We'll find out soon enough if there's any change."

Lucky caught his litter-sister's eye as they turned and padded back toward their camp. There was anxiety in Bella's expression. *She's no more certain of this than I am,* he thought.

But at least Bella was keeping the Pack's spirits up, and it made Lucky happy to watch them turning their ritual circles and sending their thoughts to the Sky-Dogs. He felt a little more optimistic as he settled to sleep himself, his head against his litter-sister's warm flank.

They were trying to connect with the ways of the Wild. If they were going to survive in this empty and broken world, they were going to have to learn to understand it the same way that Lucky had learned to understand the city.

It was going to take time, he knew. But as no-sun approached, Lucky felt a flutter of hope.

Maybe they can learn, he thought.

A crash woke him from a deep sleep. As Lucky jerked his head, his whole body tensing and bristling, he felt the spatter of cold raindrops against his fur. Flattening his ears against his skull, he looked up just in time to see a bolt of energy from Lightning's hindpaws crackle across the blackness of no-sun. The Sky-Dogs snarled again.

Beside him, Bella snapped awake, trembling. The others too were waking up, whining anxiously as rain began battering their bodies. Lucky cringed at the drops, which felt as hard as stones falling from the sky. Within a few seconds his fur was plastered to his skin. Again Lightning leaped, and this time the Sky-Dogs gave an enormous deafening growl directly above them.

Sunshine sprang to her feet, yelping and barking now, and the rest followed. Lucky stood in the center of the panicking Pack, turning on the spot to watch them and beginning to get dizzy as they ran in chaotic circles.

"What's wrong? Stop! Slow down!"

"A storm, Lucky!" howled Daisy. "We need to hide!"

Lucky barked his reassurance, but they took no notice of him. Even Bruno, usually so stolid, was whimpering as he dashed from tree to tree.

"It's just a storm!" It was certainly a fierce one, but Lucky knew he had to calm them down. He tried a jovial bark. "You're Wild Dogs now; you don't have to be scared of Lightning and the Sky-Dogs' bickering."

"But Sunshine's right," yelped Martha, pressing her body close to the ground as Lightning's bolt of power exploded yet again over their heads. "There's nowhere to shelter! Where do we run to?"

They were panicking. Lucky could understand—their longpaws must have protected them from every storm, coddling them in their baskets and kennels whenever Lightning bounded across the sky, whenever the Sky-Dogs tussled noisily. He'd gotten them through a storm before, but it hadn't been nearly this bad. The Leashed Dogs simply weren't used to facing a true storm by themselves.

"Listen to the Sky-Dogs," wailed Mickey. "They're furious!"

"They're only growling at Lightning!" barked Lucky, but his voice was lost in another chorus of thunder from the Sky-Dogs.

Martha cowered, trying to put her huge paws over her ears. "They've sent Lightning to burn the earth. They must be angry with us!"

Sunshine was a blur of white fur, dashing here and there, whining and howling her terror. At last, exhausted, she crept between Martha's legs, shaking violently.

"It's never going to end," she whimpered. "First the Big Growl, then those horrible Fight Dogs. And now the Sky-Dogs and Lightning are trying to finish us off! We've got the most awful luck! Nothing but trouble!"

"Sunshine, calm down!" Lucky tried to lick the little dog's black nose, but she had buried her head in Martha's fur, and the older dog's own whines and trembles did nothing to settle her.

Lucky feared this was going to lead to real trouble. The Leashed Dogs were working themselves into a frenzy. Mickey was backing away, staring in terror at the sky. Martha stood up and began to lumber blindly toward the river, her wounded leg threatening to give with every step. She seemed to have forgotten Sunshine, who started to bark wildly now that her shelter had been taken away. Elsewhere, Lucky could see Bruno making a sudden, clumsy break for the open ground.

They're running! Lucky realized with horror. The Pack was splitting up. He spun around again, not knowing which dog to chase after first.

They're going to get lost, scattered . . . Lightning will burn them. . . .

And the enemy Pack is still out there!

CHAPTER FIVE

Lucky was soaked to the skin. He raised his hackles, turned up his head, and waited for a pause in the Sky-Dogs' snarling and growling. When it came, he gave the loudest, most commanding bark that he could muster.

"Come with me," he ordered. "Now."

The Leashed Dogs grew still, looking about themselves in shock. Then they crept closer to him, shivering as they moved. Lucky gave a few barks and growls of encouragement as he began to guide them toward the thicker tree cover. There might be some risk of falling trees and branches, but it would be much more dangerous to let the Leashed Dogs go on working themselves into their panic out in the open, where any stray lashing of Lightning could kill them instantly. Lucky snapped at Sunshine as she hesitated, and she jumped to follow him. Heads low, and tails between their legs, the Leashed Dogs crept into the dark undergrowth after Lucky.

The belt of trees here was dense, though it thinned out into a clearing a few dog-lengths away where a single tall pine stood alone, higher than the others. Whining reassurance, Lucky gathered the dogs into the bushiest thicket of trunks, a good leap-stride from the clearing. He didn't know why, but he felt sure they had to stay here, concealed from the Sky-Dogs.

The thicker foliage muffled the rage of the storm, and even the rain couldn't pelt down so hard. Lucky could hear his friends' breathing beginning to calm down, their whining growing quieter and more subdued. They were getting ahold of themselves. Lucky let out a huff of relief. Mickey shook his head from side to side and growled, as if realizing suddenly how silly he'd been. All of them peered nervously up through the branches at the sky, waiting for the next outburst.

Then the sky exploded into brightness. Lightning hurtled to Earth, trailing his blinding energy. Lucky froze with terror as Lightning's hindlegs caught the lone pine. It seemed to explode into flames, the ball of fire almost blindingly bright.

For an instant, the dogs were stunned into silence by the heat and the light. No-sun had been driven away by the glare and roar of the flaming tree. Lucky bit back a whine of relief and fear. *I remember! Old Hunter had seen many storms, and told me that lone trees were* always *attacked by Lightning.*

"Wildfire!" Mickey howled, tail tight between his legs.

"NO!" Any control that Sunshine had gained was torn apart, as she fled from the safety of the trees with an anguished howl.

"Sunshine!" Bella barked. "Come back!"

The little dog was already a distance away, racing toward the water. "River-Dog! River-Dog! Protect us!" she howled.

"No!" Bella sped after Sunshine, and then Lucky spotted what his litter-sister had obviously seen.

The river in front of Sunshine looked strange, like no river he had ever seen before. It looked as if it was rising, bulging. Cold horror ran through Lucky's body as he raced after Bella, barking at Sunshine to stop.

Sunshine took no notice of either of them, and continued to bolt toward the swelling river. As Lightning slashed another path across the sky, Lucky saw the danger clearly, just for an instant. The water was higher than the bank. How was that even possible? It was a dirty, foaming line, and the river was coming toward them.

With a shock as sharp as if Lightning had run right into him, he realized. *The river's breaking free!*

Bella was on top of Sunshine now, holding her down. Lucky

leaped in to help his litter-sister move the little dog. He grabbed on to one of Sunshine's forelegs while Bella took her collar between her teeth. Then they scrabbled into an abrupt turn, racing away from the looming water. Sunshine yelped—more in shock than pain—as they pulled her away.

Then Lucky heard the sudden crash and roar of the water. *So much for liking the stick; the River-Dog is furious!*

They burst into the trees as the other dogs stared past them, their eyes wide and their flanks heaving in horror. As he and Bella dropped Sunshine unceremoniously to the ground, Lucky spun on his paws.

The river was still rushing toward them, the clear water turned to a churning darkness. The River-Dog was baying his rage. The waves of water were racing closer, their tips edged with that sick-looking, creamy foam.

"Run!" barked Lucky.

The dogs didn't need to be told twice. Yelping with terror, they fled farther up the valley, while behind them, the menacing torrent thundered through the trees where they'd been standing moments before. Lucky heard the tear and crack of branches pounded by water.

"Higher ground!" barked Lucky urgently. "Keep going up!"

Water could not climb hills—that much, he knew.

The dogs were panting and gasping by the time Lucky let them halt, high on the slope. Flanks heaving, they stared down at the sheet of dirty, choppy water that lay across the lower meadows. Many of the trees were half-submerged, small waves licking at their trunks.

Lucky glanced at the sky. Clouds were breaking up, letting the Moon-Dog gleam between their shreds, and the rain had slackened to a spitting drizzle. The battle above them was over, and the Sky-Dogs' rumbling growls faded in the distance. The pine was sending up clouds of sharp-scented steam, its top branches blackened, half its trunk submerged in the broken river. A few last flames flickered in its topmost branches, but Wildfire's trail had been swallowed by the water.

"It's over," breathed Martha. "The Sky-Dogs have stopped fighting."

"For now." Sunshine shivered. "I'm sorry, Lucky. I'm sorry, Bella. I didn't know what to do. I was so scared. . . ."

"Don't worry too much," said Lucky. Thinking his bark might have been a little gruff, he gave her ear a reassuring lick. "But try not to panic. Trust in your Packmates. They are who you need to rely on now."

The hillside seemed very exposed, but that didn't bother Lucky when he thought about what might have happened to them had they stayed lower down the slope. He picked his way farther up, through flattened grass and tangled twigs, letting the others follow at their own speed. They'd been barked at more than enough since his return, and any haste or urgency might cause one of them to make a wrong step in the dark. This was something they could not afford.

Still, they were close behind him when he paused on a ridge and cocked an ear. The ground fell away quite sharply, as far as a dog could safely jump, then leveled out into a shallow dip like a longpaw drinking bowl. It was sheltered, and the surface looked like it had not been wounded by the Big Growl.

"Let's sleep here," suggested Lucky.

"Is it safe?" Daisy was trembling, only partly from the exhaustion of the climb.

Lucky licked her ear. "It's as safe as it can be, I think. I doubt we'll find any other shelter up here."

"Lucky's right," agreed Bella. "Don't worry, Daisy. We'll look after you."

Lucky gave her an affectionate glance. He had a feeling that after what had happened to poor Alfie, Bella would be more protective of the smaller dogs than ever. "It'll be sunup soon. We should get a bit of extra sleep if we can."

Lucky was almost too tired to tread his ritual circle, and when he curled up by himself the tip of his tail flicked restlessly. The others soon fell into an exhausted sleep, but Lucky found he could not.

Wriggling, he tried to make himself more comfortable, but his fur was still sopping wet, and he could feel every little stone and twig against his body. He stood up to give himself an extra shake, but it didn't help much. The air was cold against his wet skin, and his ears and tail felt bedraggled and heavy.

Once more he curled on the ground, his head on his paws, and closed his eyes determinedly. *Please, Moon-Dog,* he thought. *Let me rest. . . .*

CHAPTER SIX

He must have drifted into sleep eventually, Lucky realized, because the Sun-Dog had bounded high into the sky by the time his eyes next blinked open. Rising and stretching gratefully, he gave himself a huge shake. His fur was dry at last, and he felt both warmer and much better.

The rest of the Pack was a little way down the hill, excitedly dashing along the river's new banks, sniffing at the water. Lucky stared. The river's overflow had become a lake. It had subsided quite a bit from its high point in the night, and now shone silver in the sunlight, lapping peacefully at the grass and tree trunks it had flooded.

Spotting him, Daisy barked a joyful "Good morning!" and bounded up the hill to jump and nip at his muzzle.

"Come and see, Lucky. You won't believe what we've found!"

"What is it, Daisy?" He could hear the fondness in his own voice. He was glad the little white dog was happy again. She trotted down the slope ahead of him, tail wagging, and for a moment Lucky thought with alarm that she was going to plunge straight into the river. But she stopped right on its new edge, where it had eaten away the bank, and turned to face him again, panting happily.

Lucky peered past her, puzzled. "What is it?"

Bruno padded to his shoulder. "No, Lucky—*there*. Beneath the bank. The river must have washed away some loose earth. And look what it has uncovered!"

Still doubtful, Lucky dropped carefully to a flat patch of sand. He looked closer. Bruno was right—the rising water had washed away rocks, roots, and soil, revealing deep caves in the rock.

"That is amazing." Lucky padded closer, sniffing at the great holes. They looked as if a gigantic dog had scooped them out of the high bank. Lucky frowned, thinking this must have been a very careful dog, because all the holes looked the same. Each one was as high as a fully grown longpaw, and the walls inside were of smooth stone, dry and clean and . . .

Unnatural.

His flanks tingled as memories drifted through his mind. Uncomfortable memories of rooms in the Trap House—long cold-rooms between the cage-rooms—but these caves were smaller, and of course there were no cages inside them.

They did look like excellent shelters. . . .

"The River-Dog must have done this," announced Martha. "He wasn't angry last night at all. He answered us, and dug these holes for us to hide in. Your idea worked, Mickey!"

"Thanks to you, Martha," he said a little shyly.

"We asked the River-Dog for clean water," said Sunshine, "and he's given us that, too!"

Lucky cocked his head in surprise as he watched Bruno stride to the water's edge. He dipped his head toward the water, gulping happily. Then he raised his dripping muzzle to look proudly at him.

"Are you sure?" Hesitantly Lucky padded forward and sniffed. "It does smell a bit better," he agreed. But he wasn't sure the river was entirely pure yet. There was a lot more water after the storm, and it had spread. Maybe the poison was hiding, preparing to come back and strike them later?

He wouldn't give voice to his doubts for now. It was nice to see the Leashed Dogs looking happy and confident after their terror in the storm. Their certainty in the River-Dog's help could do nothing but good for their mood.

Martha plunged into the water, right up to her shoulders,

looking delighted to have a chance to swim once more and bathe her injured leg. Daisy and Sunshine watched happily from the shallows, less inclined to fling themselves in. Leaving them to their high-spirited splashing and lapping, Lucky wandered back to the exposed caves.

Bella came quietly to his side, sniffing and gazing at the great holes with him. "They look like they might be useful," she murmured. "But I'm not sure I'd want to stay in them for very long."

"Just what I was thinking," Lucky agreed. "After all, there's no saying the river can't rise again. If it does, it might wash away anything inside these caves."

"Just like it washed away the mud that was here," said Bella with a shiver.

"Still, they'll make a good temporary camp." Lucky ventured inside one, and pawed gently at the wall, leaving shallow scratch-marks. "It will do the others good to rest for a while."

"Yes." Bella averted her eyes. "I'm sorry about what happened during the Sky-Dogs' fight, Lucky. We . . . I panicked."

Lucky nodded. There seemed to be nothing to say. Bella obviously understood how dangerous their pointless frenzy had been. She'd know to stay calm next time, he thought. At least, he hoped so. "I wonder where you should go after this though, Bella—" He froze, interrupted by a dreadful sound: a sickening, choking, heaving growl. As he and Bella turned, another guttural noise rattled his ears—a monstrous retching.

"What is—"

"Bruno!" Bella cried.

As they bolted toward him, the thickset dog gave one last ghastly heave, spewing thick, evil-smelling chunks from his mouth. Then he collapsed onto his side, his paws flailing weakly. The rest of the Pack crowded around, and Lucky shouldered his way through, shoving them aside. Standing over Bruno, he stared down in horror. The burly dog's lips had turned a ghastly color, and lumps of the foul chunks clung to his mouth and gasping jaws. He was drooling nasty-smelling foam. His breaths made it sound as though his throat was twisted and knotted.

There's rottenness inside him! thought Lucky, feeling a burn of dread in his body. *Like a spoil-box—but a living one!*

He knew what to do, although he had never done it before. Lucky lunged for the struggling dog, slamming his head into Bruno's heaving belly. Before the others could object, he did it again. Then the Pack was pawing at him, yelping and barking.

"Lucky, don't!"

"Leave him alone! What are you doing?"

Shaking them off, Lucky growled and head-butted Bruno again, making the dog thrash and squirm. Again and again he slammed his skull into Bruno's gut, ignoring the protests.

Then Bruno gave a great, retching cough, spraying more foul chunks from his mouth. The mess hit the ground like rain as the sick dog's head lolled back.

Lucky drew back, trembling. Bruno's eyes had lost their glazed, dead look, but he didn't stir from the ground, and his weak breathing was still a horrible hacking rasp.

"What was that?" whispered Bella. "Lucky, what did you do to him?"

Lucky shook his head. "The sickness had to come out of him, and that was the only way to do it. Old Hunter told me the secret. I never had to use it until now."

Daisy looked stunned. "But what—what would it have done to him?"

"It can kill a dog," said Lucky. "But not if he spits it out. Haven't you heard of this?"

The others exchanged embarrassed glances, and Lucky sighed. "No," he said. "Your longpaws would just take you to that vet of yours, wouldn't they? The longpaw-healer?"

"Yes." Mickey seemed dazed, too. "It's a good thing you were here, Lucky."

Bella nuzzled him gratefully. "It is. Or we'd have been giving Bruno to the Earth-Dog along with Alfie."

"Bruno's still very sick," Lucky pointed out, as Bruno tried and failed to lift his great fierce head. "We'll have to take care of him for a while." He added quietly to Bella alone, "And Martha's leg is still healing. Which means we should not be doing any difficult traveling, anyway."

Bella whined in agreement. "That's true. But what made Bruno so sick?"

"It must have been the water he drank."

"I was afraid of that." Bella's head dipped for just a moment, but Lucky's litter-sister was not going to be sad for too long. She picked it up again and addressed the Pack. "Everyone, remember you mustn't drink the river-water. It is still not safe for dogs."

The atmosphere was subdued as the others slowly dispersed to investigate their new, temporary territory. Lucky wished there was something he could say to make them all feel better, but what could that be? Without him, they would not have a chance of surviving at all. As long as they needed him, he would have to stay.

However long it takes, he promised himself.

"Lucky! Bella!"

Daisy had wandered away, unwilling to watch poor Bruno's agony, but now her bark was urgent.

What now? thought Lucky, as a thrill of fear rippled through his skin. If they were under attack, with Bruno so sick and vulnerable, and Martha injured, they were in big trouble. . . .

CHAPTER SEVEN

Lucky's tense muscles sagged with relief as he turned to see Daisy's head sticking out of one of the caves. She looked a little excited but unafraid.

"Look in here, quick!" she barked. "And bring Bruno. There's clean water—really clean. There's a sort of bowl in the rock, and some rain has gathered."

"Well spotted, Daisy," said Bella. "Now let's get Bruno into the cave. You too, Martha. You need to rest that leg."

With some difficulty they managed to drag Bruno's limp bulk into the cave; his claws scrabbled on the cave floor as he tried to help them, but to little effect. Once inside, they managed to roll Bruno onto his belly so that he could lap at the pure rainwater. Only when he and Martha had drunk their fill did the others line up to do the same.

Mickey poked his black-and-white nose out of the cave. His ears were pricked high with excitement. "Lucky, come and see what I've found!"

Lucky trotted over curiously to where Mickey was nosing at small objects on the cave floor. He heard Bella walking after him.

Mickey's eyes were shining brightly. "Do you see?"

"I'm not sure." Lucky wished he could be as enthusiastic as Mickey, if only to make the whole day more cheerful for everyone, but all he could do was paw at a piece of twisted metal, cocking his head to the side. "What are they?"

"Bella, you see it, don't you?" Mickey nudged a stone bowl, making it roll and clatter to Bella's feet. "These are longpaw things!"

Bella cocked her head and gave a happy bark. "You're right! Look, here's one of those skin covers that they would put over their bottom paws before they went for walks." She picked it up delicately in her teeth and showed it to Lucky.

"So what?" asked Lucky, bewildered. "We're not very far from the city—"

"Don't you see?" yelped Mickey. "When the water washed the mud away, and showed us all this—it wasn't the River-Dog at all. It was our longpaws—they're still watching over us!"

Lucky gave a soft growl of disapproval. He hadn't always been very good at keeping in touch with the Spirit Dogs, and sometimes he'd been less than respectful, but what Mickey was saying sounded like an outright insult to the River-Dog.

Still, the others didn't seem to notice that. They were beginning to crowd around Mickey. Martha, still favoring her injured leg, limped over as fast as she could. When she'd had a thorough sniff at the longpaw relics, she confirmed exactly what Lucky had been thinking.

"You shouldn't doubt the River-Dog, Mickey," she said. "He's been good to us."

"He made Bruno sick," grunted Mickey, but he didn't meet her eyes.

"I'm not sure either." Daisy sat back on her haunches, inspecting Mickey's haul. "If our longpaws were near, wouldn't they come to get us?"

"Maybe they can't," objected Mickey, gathering the longpaw things into a tidy pile. He had moved his own longpaw glove to lie with them, Lucky noticed. "Maybe this is their way of telling us they still care, even though they can't come for us. And they've given us shelter, and water! See? Even the hollow in the floor looks like my old longpaw bowl that they gave me to drink from!"

"I've never heard such nonsense," muttered Lucky, and Sunshine and Daisy gave him uncertain looks.

"And I still trust in the River-Dog!" declared Martha firmly.

But Mickey showed no sign of being swayed by her argument. "They're protecting us," he growled, "and they're watching over us. That means they'll come back!"

"Oh, Mickey—do you really think so?" Sunshine yipped.

Daisy barked excitedly. "Perhaps it is true! Yes, maybe the longpaws still want to keep us safe!"

Lucky shook his head as the two small dogs bounced and yapped with happiness. They clearly wanted to believe that Mickey was right, that the longpaws were looking after them even from far away. He sighed to himself. There seemed to be no convincing these Leashed Dogs that they were on their own now. He might have said this out loud, but Bella nudged his shoulder before he could.

"Come with me, Lucky," she said softly. "While the others are distracted. There's something I want you to see."

Lucky paced after his litter-sister as she led him out of the caves and away from their camp. There was a thin copse of trees a few paces up from the bank, where the ground was soft and wet.

"Here." Bella stopped and sat down, nodding her head at something on the ground. She looked very solemn—almost afraid.

Lucky bent his nose to the paw prints. He felt a shiver of nerves, and couldn't help jerking his head back, but then he sniffed again.

The paw prints were from a small dog, and that at least was reassuring. What was more worrying was that they seemed fresh, as if they'd been made only hours ago, but try as he might, Lucky could pick up almost no scent at all, just the smell of river-water. He took the deepest breath through his nostrils that he possibly could, but still there was nothing.

The print had not been made by one of his own Pack, but that was all Lucky could figure out.

It's as if some kind of ghost dog has passed by, he thought.

But ghost dogs did not leave prints in the mud. Lucky shook his head and growled with frustration. He had no idea if the dog was still close, even, or if it was long gone and far away.

So perhaps they had better not hang around. . . .

"Lucky, I'm scared." Bella, beside him, echoed his own thoughts too closely, and his neck prickled.

"There are other dogs nearby," he said. "That's for sure."

"Bruno has been poisoned, and Martha is still hurt. Our two best fighters. And even if no one else drinks the river-water, they will probably still get sick from having nothing to drink at all! There isn't enough water gathering in that cave—if it doesn't rain tonight, we'll be right back where we started. And we haven't hunted for a while. We're going to need food soon!"

This wasn't just Bella's cry of despair, Lucky realized; there was the gleam of an idea in his litter-sister's eye. With a sense of foreboding, he licked his chops. "What are you suggesting?" he asked her.

Bella lay down on her forepaws. She gazed up at him with determined eyes. "We have to get to that other Pack's water supply. And we have to be able to share it. We have to have water, and we have to be allowed to hunt in this valley!"

This was typical Bella thinking, thought Lucky, half in admiration and half in sheer irritation. His litter-sister always wanted to do the impossible thing, always sure she could have her way by sheer force of will. Stalling for time, he gave the prints another sniff.

Still nothing.

"Bella," he told her, trying to keep his tone as reasonable as possible. "Don't you remember what happened to Alfie?"

"Of course I do!"

"Then *think*!" he yelped. "The dogs in that Pack aren't going to change their minds just because one of us has fallen sick! All that means to them is there's one less dog that they have to fight!"

Bella glanced over her shoulder, as if checking to make sure no one else had come close. When she turned back, her eyes had that stubborn look he dreaded. "And that's exactly why we need to insist on *sharing* the lake and the hunting."

"No—it's why you need to get away from here. That Pack is vicious and ruthless. There is no way you will ever persuade them to share their territory. That's how Packs work in the Wild. Bella, you have to figure out how to tell when you're picking a fight you can't win."

Her lips curled back over her teeth. "I won't let them drive us away. We've survived this long, out in the wild without any longpaws to take care of us! I won't give up now. We can do this."

"But you don't need to be so stubborn!" Lucky didn't want to lose his temper with her, so he concentrated for a few moments on scraping sandy earth across the mysterious paw prints. He didn't want anyone else seeing them and panicking. "You wouldn't be letting them drive you away. You'd be steering clear of them so that they won't kill you and the others. You would be making the *smart* decision."

"No." Bella's face had that stubborn look about it, the one Lucky remembered from their days in the Pup-Pack. "This time it'll be different."

Lucky barked at her. *"How?"*

She didn't avert her eyes from his. "Because now, we will go in with a *plan*. Last time I couldn't think straight to argue properly with that Pack leader. But I will make him listen to me."

"He won't wait to listen," Lucky growled through his own bared teeth. "He will just drive you off, no questions asked or answered. That's if he doesn't kill you first."

"No." Bella sat up, staring directly at him. "I said I had a plan, and I do. It's a good one, Lucky."

"Don't be ridiculous—"

"One of us needs to infiltrate that other Pack," she interrupted. "To become a member, so that they can speak for us as one of them. Do you see now, Lucky?"

There was triumph in her voice, and Lucky let out a low growl.

"The other Pack never laid eyes on you, because you weren't in the fight." Bella paused, her eyes narrowing as she stared at him. "Because you had left us."

Lucky's jaws clenched. Part of him resented that Bella was trying to make him feel bad about that, but another part of him felt that she was right to be angry with him. After all, he had his own guilty secret. How could he explain to her that one of the dogs from that other Pack had seen him? And that this dog knew *exactly* who he was, and maybe even knew him as well as Bella did?

There was no way to explain this to his litter-sister now, not without raising questions to which Lucky was not sure he had the answers. Perhaps if he had told them at the very beginning, when he found Bella and the others under that tangle of roots, but now?

Impossible.

Lucky fell silent, torn by conflicting loyalties, but Bella seemed not to notice his sudden unease. He could sense her hide prickling in excitement as she pondered her plans, her tail thumping the ground enthusiastically.

"You'll make friends with them," she continued. "You'll earn their trust. You're good at making dogs like you. Once they do, you'll be able to get them to let us share their water. If that doesn't work, you're clever enough to find a way for us to get at the lake without them realizing! It's a good plan, Lucky!"

"It's a crazy plan," he grumbled. "How long do you expect me to spy for you?"

"Oh . . . just until we're back to our full strength," she told him airily. "When Martha's leg has healed and Bruno's feeling better, we can make our move—if the other Pack still doesn't want us here, we'll be able to go somewhere else. It's only for now, Lucky. You know how desperate we are. You will do it, won't you?" She looked at him with pleading eyes.

Would he? He hated the idea. He didn't want to be a spy; he

didn't want to pretend he was something he was not. But if he refused Bella's request, he would be letting down his litter-sister, and the rest of the Leashed Dogs.

If he agreed, he would have to deceive Sweet.

Bella was right. Martha and Bruno *needed* food and water and a place to rest, and how else were they going to get it? And there was no other member of Bella's Pack who could do this. Not only was he the only dog the Wild Pack hadn't seen, Lucky was the only one of them who had a chance of succeeding.

He was a cunning street dog.

Lucky sighed and sat down, ears drooping. "Yes, Bella. I'll do it. You know I will."

"Great," said Bella. "Now, I spotted something before that other Pack attacked us. Farther up the valley—about five or six rabbit-chases—there's an old longpaw camp. It's just like the ones I used to go to sometimes, with my own longpaws. They went there to play and eat—you know, there were places for dogs to chase balls, and wooden tables, and big pits where the longpaws made fire."

"No, I *don't* know," Lucky reminded her, thinking of the longpaws he'd seen playing in the city parks with their pups, their food baskets, and their ball games. Would he be running the risk of encountering any longpaws? The only ones he had seen since he left the city were those with the yellow-fur, and they hadn't seemed interested in dogs at all.

"Oh, don't look so alarmed, Lucky!" said Bella. "It's long abandoned."

Lucky cocked his head doubtfully. "How can you tell?"

"All the longpaw things had been broken up by the first Big Growl, and nobody's come to fix them. You can't miss it," Bella went on. "You'll smell old fires and burned food, and longpaws. I'll go there every night, as soon as the Moon-Dog rises, and I will wait for you until he's right overhead. As soon as there's a no-sun when you think it's safe, slip away from that Pack and meet me there so you can tell me what you have learned."

Lucky let his head dip slowly to show that he agreed. If Bella wanted to go ahead with her outlandish plan, this did seem like the safest way to do it. "All right. Every no-sun, wait for me there. I'll come as soon as I can."

She licked his nose. "Thank you, Lucky! I knew you would help us."

Without another word she turned and trotted back toward the camp, tongue lolling, head and tail held high. His litter-sister looked like a real Alpha now. The trouble was, she didn't yet have a Pack leader's wisdom or wiles, only impulsive schemes. He couldn't blame her—she was doing her best, and she wasn't used to this life—but he was worried she would plot herself into big trouble before long.

With a sigh, Lucky padded after her, feeling a tingling ball of nerves in his belly. He was a clever dog—sneaky and cunning and crafty, he thought, remembering uneasily what their Mother-Dog would have had to say about that—but surviving in the city was so different from life in the wild. In the city, if he had tried to steal food from longpaws, he would have been chased off. If he got away, he was safe—free and clear. Longpaws eventually gave up and went back to their homes.

If the dog-wolf caught him trying to cheat his Pack, thought Lucky, he wouldn't just chase Lucky away. Lucky would be in real danger.

CHAPTER EIGHT

"There! A mouse!" Daisy shot off after the little rodent, her burst of speed bringing her swiftly on top of it. With a snap of her jaws, she tossed it into the air, limp and broken, caught it, and brought it proudly back to Lucky.

"Well done, Daisy!" She was turning into a natural. Prey had been hard to find this morning, and Lucky suspected the torrential storm had drowned or driven away much of what the Big Growl had left behind.

The Sun-Dog was racing higher and ever swifter into a clear blue rain-washed sky, which meant the best time for hunting was over—but Lucky found himself reluctant to give up and return to the caves. Daisy had caught their third mouse, and Mickey had surprised a fat brown bird dozing on a low branch, but it would be good to get something more—and besides, Lucky was almost dreading the end of this hunt.

This sun-high would be when he would leave the Leashed

Dogs and try to wrangle his way into the enemy Pack, and even the thought of seeing Sweet again couldn't make him feel any better.

A bird scolded the dogs from high up in a pine, too far away for Lucky to do anything more than give it his best threatening glare. Soon there would be nothing to hunt but beetles and bugs, and then he would have no excuses. Stopping to sniff the air, Lucky saw Mickey slinking through the trees off to his left, low to the ground. Another ripple of pride went through his blood.

"Look!" cried Daisy. A rabbit leaped from the grass almost at Mickey's feet, hurtling toward Lucky in a panic and swerving aside at the last moment. Sunshine cut it off and drove it back toward Lucky, but it was Mickey who intercepted it with an agile sideways leap, and his jaws crunched down on its spine.

"Well done, Mickey!" Sunshine was jumping up and down and spinning with excitement.

"You did well too, Sunshine," Lucky pointed out, giving her ear a lick. "This was a real team effort!"

The little dog looked about to burst, and Lucky remembered with amusement her early dislike of hunting, her fear of getting her beautiful white fur caught on twigs. Now she looked grubby and her coat was matted, but she bounced with pride.

There was no putting off the moment anymore; their haul of prey was excellent for such an unpromising sunup. Lucky barked to bring the others back to him. Then, together, they carried their kills back to Martha, Bruno, and Bella.

They weren't quite in sight of the river and caves when Lucky halted, a scent bringing him up short. His hackles rose as he stood stiff-legged, sniffing the still air.

"Lucky? What is it?" Sunshine laid down her mouse and looked up at him quizzically.

"Nothing, I hope," he growled softly. "You three go on. I'm going to do a quick scout around here."

Sunshine looked uncertain, but obediently picked up her mouse and trotted toward the caves with Mickey and Daisy.

Lucky waited until they were out of sight over a slight rise, then lowered his muzzle to the ground, his sense of threat making his coat bristle all over. He hadn't wanted to say anything to the others, not yet; but he was certain of it. . . .

A Fierce Dog had passed this way.

It couldn't have been one of the enemy Pack led by the dog-wolf. Lucky hadn't seen any of those sleek black Fierce Dogs among them, and besides, there was something familiar about this particular scent. A picture came to his mind as the smell filled his nostrils: the strange doghouses where the Leashed Dogs had been caught and imprisoned by the violent Fierce Dog Pack. If Lucky had not been there to help them, he remembered with a shudder, Bella, Daisy, and Alfie would have probably been torn to pieces.

A nervous whine escaped Lucky's lips. Surely the Fierce Dogs would not pursue them all the way here, just for revenge for their wounded pride? The female Alpha, Blade, had been especially arrogant and savage, but would she really leave her easy, spoiled existence in the Dog-Garden to come after a Pack of mangy Leashed Dogs?

Lucky wasn't sure. And, in a way, that was worse than having something terrible but definite to fear.

He took his time snuffling around the trees, using his nose to nudge aside stones and branches. At last he felt a little more reassured—the scents were old and had not been refreshed recently, so whoever the Fierce Dog was, he had just been passing through. Still, he felt uneasy as he followed the others back toward the caves. There were far too many signs of danger around this place, too many traces of unfriendly dogs. Bella and her Pack could only move forward now. They could not turn around and walk back the way they had come—not when they were caught between two fierce, hostile Packs.

They needed to find a territory all their own. *Somewhere.*

The others were waiting for him, so happy and excited at the prospect of a good meal that Lucky decided not to mention his misgivings, or tell them about the strange and alarming Fierce Dog scent he had picked up. Any apprehension he felt was defeated by his appetite, which had been sharpened by the hunt and the clear air. He fell on his share of the prey with enthusiasm.

Afterward, he sprawled in the Sun-Dog's light and heat, his belly full and his ears tickled by the soft breathing and contented grunts of his friends. At last, he rose up to all fours, stretching and shaking himself from head to tail. Much as he would have liked to, there was no sense putting this off any longer. As he paced toward Bella, the others raised their heads and got to their feet one by one, nervously gathering around him.

"I should be going." Lucky nuzzled Bella's ear, wanting to stay angry with her, but too aware of how much he would miss her, as well as the safety and companionship of this odd Pack, while he was away on his dangerous mission.

"I wish you didn't have to go," said Daisy.

"We've only just got you back," Sunshine whined. "And those other dogs are so scary. Are you sure you'll be safe?"

Lucky licked her black nose. "It's for the best. You have to trust in Bella and me. That's what Pack's all about." He wished he felt half as confident as he sounded. "I'll be back again soon, and by that time I hope we will have clean water to drink. I'll do my best for you all."

"We know you will, Lucky." Mickey nuzzled his neck. "Just . . . be careful."

Suppressing a shudder, Lucky wagged his tail cheerfully. "Of course I will." He turned to give Bella a last glance.

She was watching him with a solemn look in her dark eyes. More and more, he thought, she seemed to fit naturally into her role as Alpha, and more and more he wished he could be sure she was capable of this responsibility. All the same he licked her nose fondly and pressed his face to hers before forcing himself to turn away and begin his journey.

He did not look back as he bounded up the valley's steep side. The air was warming rapidly, and he panted with the exertion, but he wanted to follow a high route toward the shining lake so that he would not be vulnerable to surprise attacks. There could be other dogs in the valley besides the enemy Pack.

He was glad his belly was full, because his thoughts were focused on what lay ahead, not on hunting. The prey seemed to know it, too; birds sang cheekily close to him and a mouse had the confidence to scuttle across his path and under a log. Lucky was not altogether sure if his anxiety was due to the angry enemies ahead or the thought of seeing Sweet again.

He almost wished the other Pack's guards would make their appearance so that he could stop worrying. The land was evening out, and as he crested a small ridge he saw the lake spilling away before him, brilliantly reflecting the Sun-Dog's shine. Surely, now . . .

There! Lucky jerked his head up at the sound of a ferocious bark, just as three dogs leaped out to confront him. Even as his hackles rose instinctively, Lucky felt a strange flutter of relief.

"What are you doing here?" A lean brown-and-white chase-dog, like a smaller swift-dog, stood squarely in front of him, baring her teeth. "This is our territory!"

Our territory! Lucky remembered their savage barks and howls on the day Alfie died. *Ours!*

"Leave this place now," snarled a long-eared black-and-tan dog. "Or face the consequences."

Lucky forced himself to hold his ground; if he turned tail, they might well chase him down and maul him, or worse. He crouched, keeping his haunches high and his forepaws low. He swung his tail nervously to signal that he was not here to threaten or challenge them on their territory.

"In the name of the Forest-Dog, I want to talk to your Alpha!" he barked.

The brown-and-white dog drew back her muzzle in a contemptuous snarl. "Why?"

Lucky took a deep breath and lowered his head even farther. He disliked bowing before these Pack Dogs. They had attacked his friends, and killed one of them! But he had no choice. And besides . . .

"Sweet the swift-dog is one of your Pack," he said. "We survived together in the city, after the Big Growl."

"And?" sneered another long-eared dog, a female who looked so much like the male that Lucky wondered if they were littermates.

He cocked his ears and let his tongue loll. If it worked for Food House longpaws, maybe his charm would even work on these dogs. "I want to join your Pack. Take me to Sweet and she'll vouch for me."

"Why would we want you in our Pack?" The brown-and-white dog's voice was full of disdain.

"Because I'm a hunter," Lucky replied. "I can be useful to you."

"We don't need scavenger city dogs who think they can hunt."

Something about the female long-ear's bearing sparked a memory in Lucky's mind—he'd seen this dog during the fight, following the Alpha's orders. This was the one the dog-wolf had called Spring.

Lucky clenched his teeth against a snarl. He knew he mustn't rise to the taunts, however tempting it was. "I would be valuable to your Pack. You would be stronger with me on your side."

To Lucky's relief, the male long-ear looked up at the brown-and-white chase-dog uncertainly. "I don't know, Dart. If he does know Sweet . . ."

"I doubt it, Twitch," snarled Dart, and turned back to Lucky. "I can smell the stink of the city on you. What is it you hunt? Food wrappers?"

The three dogs laughed scornfully. Lucky tried not to show how close the barb had come to the truth. He'd learned a lot since those days, after all. Besides, he was secretly pleased to hear that the city's stench still clung to him. It told him he was still his old self, still a City Dog and a Lone Dog.

He was still Lucky.

His quiet pleasure was shattered when the dogs began to advance again. Still refusing to back away, Lucky flattened his whole body against the ground, but he couldn't stop his muzzle from curling. If they insisted on attacking, he would fight back. Even if it only made things worse for himself.

I may still smell of it, he thought despairingly, *but I'm a long way from the city now. And I don't have any friends here. . . .*

There was no sign of these dogs giving any ground, he realized. And there was no point submitting if they were simply going to tear him to bits anyway. Baring his teeth in a warning snarl, he leapt abruptly to his feet, standing stiff and tall.

I won't be easy pickings. . . .

The male black-and-tan called Twitch was limping slightly, and Lucky was bigger than each of them, but he knew he couldn't outfight three brutal dogs all at the same time.

"Take him, Spring!"

The female black-and-tan went for him, charging low for his neck. She moved with unexpected speed, and Lucky just managed to leap sideways. But this only took him into the path of Dart, who lunged for his scruff. Lucky yelped as he felt her teeth sink into his flesh, and then Twitch sneaked in and bit his foreleg. Lucky squirmed, throwing Dart off, snarling and gnashing at Twitch.

But now Spring was back. She seized a mouthful of his neck fur and gave it a fierce tug.

Were they actually planning to kill him? Lucky didn't think

so, but they were certainly going to hurt him badly—make sure he fled and never returned. And if he couldn't get the upper paw against these three mangy brutes, there was no way he would ever get into their Pack. The rest wouldn't dream of accepting him— even Sweet.

Sharp fangs sank into his flank and he howled with pain and rage, twisting to snap at his attacker but only catching her ear. At the same time, the black-and-tan male got a grip on Lucky's own ear, tearing at it. Lucky felt a sharp pain and warm blood spreading through the fur over his skull. Dart still had hold of his neck fur, her teeth now sinking into Lucky's flesh.

Lucky felt panic begin to overwhelm him along with the rage. She was going to do serious damage if he could not shift her soon.

"Enough! LEAVE HIM!"

The bark sounded savage, but also familiar. Lucky stumbled when he felt the pressure and pain at his neck fade away. Still snarling, his three attackers backed off, their hackles bristling and their teeth bared.

Panting, Lucky gave them a defiant snarl in return, but his eyes hungrily sought out the newcomer. That scent he knew so well tickled his nostrils, and his heart thudded hard and slowed as he caught his breath.

"Sweet," he gasped.

She did not bound forward to greet him, but simply stood there, her head held high as she studied him with narrowed eyes. Her ears pricked forward and she sniffed imperiously at the air around him.

"He's an invader!" Dart barked.

"So I see." Sweet stood very still, cocking her head only slightly, never taking her eyes off Lucky.

"We were trying to get rid of him," snarled the limping male, Twitch.

"You should let us finish!" said Dart.

"No," Sweet growled. "I know this dog."

Dart lowered her head and tail. She looked submissive, and not happy about it.

"I'm going to take him to Alpha. Any objections?" Sweet looked around her Packmates, clearly not expecting any disagreement—and none came. "I shall propose him as a new member. He would be an asset to the Pack."

"Yes, Beta." The others were deferential now, though they shot venomous glances at Lucky.

Beta? Lucky thought. He knew that every Wild Pack had an Alpha, a leader, and an Omega, who had the lowest rank in the

Pack—but what was a Beta? *Just how well has Sweet settled in to this pack?* But this wasn't the time to start questioning her. "Thank you, Sweet," he began as he scrambled back on all fours. "I'll—"

"That's enough." Any warmth in Sweet's eyes was gone altogether, and a faint shiver of apprehension went through Lucky's bones.

"Sweet, I'm sorry—"

"Just follow me. And don't use my name. In fact, don't say another word."

CHAPTER NINE

Sweet led Lucky around the shore of the lake into a deep bay fringed thickly with trees. Under the branches the light was green and cool, the ground soft underpaw. After the dazzling sun-high brightness of the valley, Lucky's eyes took a little time to adjust to the shade as he followed Sweet's narrow hindquarters closely through two lines of straight trunks.

Where the trees opened out to the shallow dip of a clearing, Sweet paused. The Sun-Dog's light pierced the pine canopy here, sending spears of dusty light to the grassy ground, and Lucky could see several distinct hollows strewn with soft leaves and moss—proper sleeping dens, carefully arranged. It was a long way from the rough camps his own Pack had managed to set up.

Still, he had a feeling that comfort was not the only advantage of this camp. On most of its edges it was hemmed in by thick thorn scrub that would be impossible for any large animal to penetrate without giving themselves away. Even Daisy would struggle to make her way through this dangerous undergrowth. Lucky would have liked to stand at Sweet's side, but he respectfully held back by her flank, constantly aware of the three smaller dogs at his rear who blocked his escape route. One of the shafts of sunlight fell onto a large flat rock near the center of the clearing, warming the hide of the huge sleeping dog-wolf. Of course the most prominent part of the camp, and the warmest, had been reserved for the ferocious Alpha.

Lucky held his breath, while Sweet casually swished her tail. Three more dogs had come forward to greet her, and to sniff suspiciously at him. One was the huge brown dog he remembered from the fight, almost as big as Martha but without her gentle face. The others were a tan-and-white smaller dog and a long-eared, shaggy-furred black dog with soulful eyes but a nasty expression.

"Who is this?" growled the big dog, snuffing the air. "Don't tell me it's another of those pathetic Leashed Dogs."

Lucky bristled at the insult but he stayed quiet. The Forest-Dog would think him stupid, and unworthy of protection, if he lost his temper in this situation. But he wasn't going to cringe. If he showed too much submission, a dog as arrogant and powerful as this might simply kill him for fun.

Sweet was not intimidated, even though the black dog was nearly twice her size. She gave him an imperious twist of her muzzle. "He's with me, Fiery. Do you have a problem with that? If so, we can take it up with Alpha."

The huge dog glowered, but he clearly did not want to take his argument to Alpha. Before he could say anything, the nearby undergrowth rustled.

Lucky flinched aside as a female black-and-white Farm Dog— not unlike Mickey—poked her nose out of the scrub. "What's the commotion? My pups are trying to sleep."

"I'm sorry, Moon." The old softness was back in Sweet's voice as she lowered her nose to the Mother-Dog's. "Go back to your pups. We'll try to be quiet."

"I'm sorry, too, Moon." It shocked Lucky to hear the massive Fiery apologize so meekly. Clearly the Mother-Dog commanded a lot of respect around here.

"Well, since I'm here . . ." Moon stretched out her forepaws, and Lucky caught the scent of warm milk and squirming pups. "I'm very hungry; the pups are growing fast. Someone get me some food, please."

Instantly Sweet turned and barked toward a little dog skulking at the edge of the clearing. "Omega! Bring food for Moon at once!"

Nervously the small dog trotted out of the shadows; he was a stocky, oddly shaped creature with tiny ears and a wrinkled face. His beady black eyes were suspicious as he paused to stare at Lucky. Something about his sly expression gave Lucky a ripple of unease in his bones.

"I said, at once," Sweet reminded the little dog darkly, and he shot off across the clearing.

Sweet didn't bother to introduce Lucky to any of the other dogs, but beckoned him forward with a haughty motion of her head. "Come. I shall present you to Alpha."

She paced forward, confident but respectful. Lucky followed with rather more reluctance, still taking in his new surroundings. The Pack was larger than Bella's, at least eight dogs strong not counting Moon and her pups. This unnerved him. Not only that—the dogs seemed very comfortably placed in this sheltered camp—the clean lake was close by and, from the scents drifting out of the trees, he could tell these woods were teeming with prey.

Even at full strength Bella's Pack would be no match for this one, so well fed, well disciplined, and strong. If the Alpha couldn't be persuaded to share, Lucky would have to convince Bella that the Leashed Dogs must move on.

"Wait here." Sweet's newly commanding voice broke into his thoughts. "Don't come forward until Alpha summons you."

Lucky stared at the dog-wolf, sprawled on his rock, nothing twitching but the very tip of his tail. Perhaps he was dreaming, or perhaps he was not quite so fast asleep as he wanted to appear. Sure enough, as Sweet approached him, one cold, yellow eye blinked open.

Lucky could hear nothing the two dogs said to each other, but Sweet did not seem meek in her leader's presence. She showed respect, but she did not act submissive. She spoke quietly, and Alpha cocked his gray ears to listen closely. At last he turned his head and stared piercingly at Lucky.

Sweet turned too. "Come here, Lucky."

Under the dog-wolf's chilly gaze, Lucky felt anger swirl in his belly as he walked slowly forward. This was the monstrous brute who had killed Alfie, and Lucky wanted to snarl at him, insult him, even to lunge and bite and let *him* know how it felt. But that would be suicide. He remembered Alfie's life force seeping away, the little body going still and cold as the Earth-Dog claimed him.

I am here to help the rest of Alfie's Pack, to save them from the same fate. I must not forget it.

Close up, Alpha looked even bigger and wilder, and his yellow eyes were extraordinarily frightening. His huge paws, with their vicious nails, were webbed like Martha's, but his savage face was nothing like hers. This, thought Lucky, was a true Wild Pack leader.

"So," the dog-wolf growled. "You want to join my Pack."

There was scorn in his voice, but Lucky kept his gaze level and brave.

"Yes," he said. "I'd be a valuable Pack member. Sweet can vouch for me."

"Yes. *Beta* already has."

That title again. And the way everyone deferred to Sweet: Did it mean she was this huge dog-wolf's second in command?

Alpha sounded bored. "I have no need of another dog in my Pack."

Lucky sensed that pleading would not have any effect on this creature. He would not respect weakness or submissiveness, yet there was no sense challenging him on his own terms.

He lowered his tail, tilting his head mischievously. "You don't need any more *ordinary* dogs, but what about one as strong and fast as me? I catch a good rabbit."

Alpha yawned widely, showing every one of his teeth. "So does

99

Mulch. And Beta can bring down a deer. But then you know that, don't you, City Dog? Since you know her so well."

There was a distinct menace in the dog-wolf's eyes now. Lucky swallowed, then let his tongue loll. "Seems to me you have a lot of brute force in this Pack. But I am *clever*. That's what comes of city life. And I can survive in the wild, too. The Forest-Dog favors me."

"Is that right?" Alpha rose up on his forepaws, stretching, muscles rippling with malevolence.

Lucky ignored the dog-wolf's tone. "I can be very useful. I can bring a fresh . . . attitude. I see things differently. That can be helpful in a Pack."

"Do not tell me what's good for my Pack," snapped Alpha, and Lucky took a backward step. He had to tread carefully.

"I would not dream of it," he said, more meekly. "I was just . . . explaining my experience. The ways I think I can help. You have such a fine Pack here, I want to be part of it."

Alpha seemed slightly mollified, but the long-eared black dog gave a shrill bark of objection.

"Throw him out, Alpha! He smells *wrong*. He stinks of long-paws and stone and metal. Chase him away!"

Alpha turned his cold eyes on the black dog. "Mulch," he

growled. "Are you telling *me* what to do?"

The massive dog called Fiery whacked a paw across Mulch's head.

Mulch yelped and ducked, backing off. "Of course not, Alpha. I was just—"

"Then keep your jaws shut. Or I will have Fiery give you a proper beating."

Lucky glanced around at the other dogs who had gathered. It was not only Mulch who cowered, subdued and scared. All of them looked terrified of Alpha, their eyes wary and nervous.

Except for the brutish Fiery. And Sweet.

Because Mulch had not tried to run away, Lucky assumed this was not unusual behavior from Alpha. Despite how harsh and cruel the dog-wolf seemed, none of his followers seemed desperate to leave. Lucky's old dislike of Packs swelled in him again. The little band of Leashed Dogs traveled together because they *wanted* to—because they knew one another, liked one another.

What was binding this Pack together?

Lucky's thoughts shattered like rain on stone when he saw Sweet leap gracefully up onto Alpha's rock to stand beside the dog-wolf. He did not smack her down or scold her, and she stood with her flanks close to his, proud and strong. If anything, Alpha seemed to stand taller in her presence.

Lucky's gut twisted with dismay and jealousy. Was Sweet the dog-wolf's mate?

His horror melted into gratitude, though, as she began to speak.

"I knew Lucky in the city," she declared. "He was my only Pack when I escaped from the Trap House, and I would be dead if it was not for him. Several times over." She paused to look at each of the Pack in turn, and let her words sink in. "He is loyal, brave, strong, and smart. He would be a fine member of this Pack. In fact I asked him to join us before. He said no." She turned her head to watch Lucky, expressionless. "If he has changed his mind, that is a piece of good fortune for us. You should welcome such a dog, not"—she gave Mulch a contemptuous twist of her muzzle— "chase him away."

Alpha gave a curt nod. "He may be all those things, Beta, but this Pack is at full strength. We don't need another dog."

"Moon will be nursing her pups for at least another full journey of the Moon-Dog. We are one good fighter short. Lucky could take Moon's place on patrols, and Spring could go back to hunting. Then you can judge for yourself what kind of Pack member Lucky'll make."

Slowly Alpha nodded again. "You talk sense as usual, Beta." She dipped her head in acknowledgment as Alpha went on. "And if you vouch for this City Dog, then he can stay for now." The cold eyes swiveled to Lucky, and Alpha's lip peeled back from his teeth. "But he must prove himself of use. If he does not succeed, we can still throw him out—with a beating for his impudence. What does the Pack say?"

Lucky watched the Wild Pack as they reacted to Alpha's decision. Despite their earlier fierceness, Dart and Twitch looked at each other and their tails quivered in agreement.

"We can use another Patrol Dog," Twitch said.

Spring muttered something Lucky didn't hear, shaking her head a little.

"I say welcome," said the small tan-and-white female beside Fiery.

"Well said, Snap," said Twitch.

Fiery stayed silent, though his face showed he wasn't at all convinced. Mulch was looking away, as if he couldn't trust himself not to earn another whack from the big dog.

Lucky let out a breath for what felt like the first time since he had arrived in the clearing, lowering his head humbly. "Thank you, Alpha."

"You'll join the Pack in the place everyone does: at the bottom, superior only to Omega. Your immediate commander is Twitch." The dog-wolf jerked his head at the limping black-and-tan dog. A smug look crossed Twitch's face.

"As you say, Alpha." Lucky faked gratitude by lowering his head even more. He had anticipated that he would join the Pack with low status, but to be placed at the very bottom—above only the Omega—was nevertheless a surprise.

He couldn't help glancing at Sweet. He couldn't think of her as Beta. He'd picked up plenty of information about the way Packs worked over the years, from Wild Dogs who came into the city, but it seemed there was still a lot he didn't understand. It was strange to realize that. He'd gotten so used to being the one in the Leashed Pack who knew about the wild . . . but he was still a City Dog who'd never had to think about rank or status before.

Still, his status was something he could work on. He was smarter than Twitch—and Mulch too, he suspected—and he was sure he could swiftly rise to something better in the hierarchy.

Something closer to Sweet's rank . . .

"While you're all gathered . . ." Alpha's bark became brusque and practical. "Make sure you keep your eyes open for that pathetic gang of Leashed Dogs. I don't want them regrouping and trying another attack. If you see them, chase them off. If they won't be chased, kill them. Understood?"

"Yes, Alpha," came the chorus of yelps and barks.

"You. Lucky. Did you see a band of Leashed Dogs on your way here?"

Lucky felt every pair of eyes fall on him, and his heart tripped and raced. Would it be wiser to admit he had run into the Leashed Dogs—even that he knew them from the city? None of that was a lie. And despite her newfound confidence and status, he felt he could still trust Sweet.

But she is Alpha's mate now. . . .

"I'm not sure." Lucky hoped his lie did not sound as obvious to their ears as it did to his. "At least, I *think* I saw them—a ridiculous bunch of useless pets?—but I have no idea where they were heading."

"Then let's find out if they're anywhere near," Alpha growled. "They tried to steal from our water supply. That won't happen again. Lucky, you go with Twitch and Dart and let them show you how we do things in this Pack. Go."

With that, the dog-wolf slumped back down onto the rock, his eyes narrowing to slits as he watched them leave. Lucky glanced back over his shoulder and noticed that the yellow eyes were still fixed on him. A tingle of apprehension went through his skin, lifting the roots of his fur.

If Alpha ever found out that he had run with the Leashed Dogs, what would happen then? How would he explain his lie? *You'll need all the guile of the Forest-Dog for that one, Lucky,* he told himself. *And even that might not save you. . . .*

Then he was troubled by a second, even more horrible thought. Sweet had vouched for him, had guaranteed his worth in front of the whole Pack—a Pack in which she had real status. What would Alpha do to her if he discovered Lucky had lied, and that she had fallen for it? If Alpha thought, perhaps, that Sweet had *deliberately* deceived him?

That she was conspiring with a dog from her old life in the city?

Lucky did not like to think about what punishments Alpha would inflict on dogs who betrayed him. He was prepared to take risks—he had done so his whole life in the city.

But he did *not* want to guide anyone else into danger.

CHAPTER TEN

"Keep up, Lucky," Twitch barked, *as* he limped hurriedly along.

Lucky felt a flash of irritation. When he had hung back to sniff right inside that hollow log, he was only being thorough—a lot more thorough than Twitch and Dart were being—and he didn't think Twitch needed to be quite so bossy. If Pack status could be changed, as he suspected, he might one day be in charge of Twitch. So it wasn't very clever of Twitch to throw his weight around now.

"Don't worry about me keeping up," said Lucky. "But do stop if you feel tired." He stopped himself from saying, *If your bad leg gives up on you.*

Twitch growled. "Careful what you say. Respect is very important in this Pack."

If that were true, Lucky thought, *you'd show more of it.*

An early mist had lifted from the lake's shoreline, revealing its brilliant glitter. Pine trees were outlined in silhouette on the distant shore; there was certainly plenty of forest, and that meant plenty of prey. Once again Lucky thought how unfair it was that this Wild Pack would not share food even when they had more than they could eat. If they would, he wouldn't be in this position of having to deceive other dogs.

As they ventured into a dense copse of pines, Lucky took care to notice not just possible dangers or likely prey, but any cover that Bella and her Pack might use, to stay unseen. He wondered if his two companions thought there was something odd about the way their new recruit was sniffing the surroundings, but they said nothing more. Neither Twitch nor the brown-and-white female Dart were as alert as they should have been.

That's just my good luck.

So far, Lucky hadn't seen anything that suggested Bella would have an easy time getting what she wanted from this Pack, but then this was only his first patrol. There was plenty of time for him to snoop around some more, although he hoped he would finish this mission quickly. He did not want to be a spy dog for long.

In his head Lucky dismissed the rocky outcrop as too obvious a hiding place, but he sniffed it over carefully for possible dangers to the Wild Pack. Lucky cast an eye back to Twitch and Dart, swallowing down an arrogant rumble.

Twitch really should be noticing how nosy I am, but he seems completely clueless. Even though they're sloppy, I shouldn't take too many chances.

"That's good, Lucky. Well done," Twitch yapped.

Lucky was dragged out of his thoughts, his ears pricking up. Twitch and Dart were both watching him with a sort of superior approval. Though his fur bristled at their smugness, he found himself relieved at the same time. Twitch's hostility was obviously melting away and, though Lucky wasn't sure why this was so, he had to admit it would make his task a lot easier.

The trees opened up and suddenly there was the lake again, shining brilliant silver in the light of the Sun-Dog. Lucky gazed, mesmerized by its glitter.

"The poison hasn't spread here," he observed.

"The river-poison?" Dart yapped. "No. Anyway, it would take a lot to make this amount of water undrinkable." There was arrogant pride in her voice, and Lucky cocked his head.

"No wonder the Leashed Dogs were desperate," he murmured.

"True." Dart laughed. "Still, that isn't our problem. You shouldn't feel sorry for them."

"They should have stayed at home doing tricks for their longpaws," agreed Twitch contemptuously. "You may be a City

Dog, Lucky, but at least you know about true dog-life, life in the wild, living by your wits and surviving. Those dogs do not *deserve* to survive."

Lucky could find no answer to that, so he dipped his muzzle to the cool, clear water and, playing for time, took a long drink. He had never truly appreciated clean water before. In this new and dangerous world, on a bright, hot sunup, there was something blissfully refreshing about a simple drink. Dart and Twitch were still bantering with each other, poking fun at Bella's Pack, but he took no notice. He did not need to hear their opinions about his friends.

"Anyway, they'll have moved on, if they know what's good for them." Dart padded along the lakeshore, sniffing, then glanced back and barked in horror. "Lucky! We do not indulge ourselves on patrol!"

Lucky lifted his dripping muzzle, astonished.

"A quick lap, that's all," said Twitch sternly. "Alpha says if we eat and drink on patrol, we will not see properly. Indulging our own appetites is disregarding our duty."

Disregarding our duty? Lucky was shocked to his core. How did these mutts ever come to think like this?

Still, as much as their attitude horrified him, Lucky didn't want to cause any trouble. He backed away from the water and followed them again. Clearly Alpha was serious about discipline—and he had to admit it was true: With his tongue lapping the clear, delicious water, and the lovely coolness of it in his throat, he had been unaware of what was going on at his back. Danger could have fallen upon him, and he would have been completely caught off guard.

"One of our Pack dogs learned that lesson recently," said Dart. "Found a rabbit corpse while he was out on patrol. Ate it himself."

Twitch shuddered. "Alpha did not take kindly to that."

Lucky felt his own skin shiver. "Which dog was this?"

"He is not in the Pack anymore. We do not mention his name." Dart seemed nervous, and she gave her coat a massive shake before she trotted on. Lucky guessed that whoever the nameless dog had been, he was not in anyone's Pack now.

"Lucky, check that hillock," commanded Twitch. "Three dogs could hide behind that rise."

He had been going to do it anyway, but Lucky kept his jaws shut and did as he was told. To be truthful, he was glad of a moment's breathing space in the wake of that story about the nameless Pack member. He could not let himself forget that he was playing a very, very dangerous game. There were chills in his spine as he shoved his muzzle into hollows, pawing aside long grass to look for anything that might be hiding, ready to attack. The sharp odor of raccoon made him tense up with alarm, but when he followed the trail a rabbit-chase or two, he realized it was too old to worry about.

He looked back toward Twitch and Dart, a strange thought tugging at his fur. When those two dogs sniffed at the air, and at the ground, their tails stayed down. Nothing they scented excited them, even though Lucky knew they *had* to be teased by the scent of prey, old and new. But they stayed calm at all times.

I don't understand that.

Loping back toward Twitch and Dart, he said, "Is there anything particular we're looking for? There are so many scents, so many traces . . ."

"Alpha wants to know about anything at all that might be a threat," Twitch replied. "Other dogs, obviously, and of course, foxes and raccoons. Sometimes there are sharpclaws, and they can be sneaky." He shivered, perhaps at the memory of an old attack; Lucky, too, knew just how much a sharpclaw scratch could sting, and how quickly the wound it left could become poisoned.

"If there's a small threat, we handle it ourselves, just the patrol," Dart grumbled. "And if we need support, I head back to the camp to gather the hunters. That's why there are always at least three dogs on patrol. There has to be one to run back while the others fight. There is no getting the better of *our* Pack. Spring was patrolling with us while Moon looked after her pups, but now you're here, so Spring can go back to hunting. More food for all of us."

"That was good work you did, Lucky," said Twitch. Lucky couldn't be sure, but he thought he saw approval in the mongrel's eyes. "I saw how thoroughly you . . . *checked*."

He's testing me, Lucky realized with some annoyance. Then it struck him why Twitch was acting like a strict but indulgent Mother-Dog.

Lucky had taken Twitch's place at the bottom of the Pack hierarchy.

Being low in this Pack's order clearly made life even harder than it had to be. Once again Lucky found himself longing for Bella's scrappy Pack. They might have needed a lot of teaching in the ways of surviving but, when it came down to it, the Leashed Dogs pulled together. They cooperated because they *cared* about one another. They shared food and tasks equally because they thought of themselves as friends and equals, not as rivals for Pack position or as possible threats. Lucky felt a sudden urge to confront Twitch and Dart, to force them to question the savage rules they were living by. He wanted to tell them that their way was not the only way, that a Pack did not *have* to exile or kill dogs just for making a single mistake in a moment of desperate hunger. . . .

But Lucky clamped his jaws together and kept his silence. It would not do to start questioning the ways of Alpha's Pack so soon after he had begged to join them.

Besides, he had not *just* pleaded to join—he had lied, too. *I'm playing tricks on these dogs—and they are not the kind of tricks my Mother-Dog would have liked.*

He could hardly lecture Twitch and Dart about friendship and honor. . . .

Ahead of him, Dart had finished a long lap of the bay and was now absently sniffing the length of a huge driftwood log. For all their talk, Lucky thought, his companions' inspection of their surroundings seemed a bit brief. Dart had barely gotten to the end of the log before she jumped down and trotted straight toward a copse of pines on a small headland. Twitch was winding through tree trunks at the forest's edge, checking the roots of each, but to Lucky's eyes he seemed more concerned with following the trees in the right order than with actually examining them properly.

Lucky took a last careful sniff at the rocks under a sandy bank, then leaped up it to join Twitch and follow him into the next stretch of woodland. "Moon would usually lead this patrol, is that right?" he asked. Alpha had said that Moon wasn't patrolling because she was caring for her pups, and the respect the other dogs treated her with made Lucky think the Mother-Dog must be higher in the Pack hierarchy than Twitch or Dart.

"Yes," Twitch replied. "When she's on patrol, nothing escapes her. She could be a hunter, but she's so good at tracking and scenting—the best in the Pack." Twitch's voice held an awe and respect that told Lucky a lot about Moon's status. "But of course she's nursing her pups now—hers and Fiery's. They are such strong dogs, that pair, and so experienced. They've been running with Alpha for a very long time."

Lucky tilted his head as he walked beside Twitch. "And has Sweet—Beta—been with him a long time too?" He was very curious to learn what had happened to his friend since he'd known her in the city. . . .

"Beta? No. She's the newest member of the Pack!" If possible Twitch's eyes grew even bigger and rounder. "She joined maybe half a Moon-Dog journey after the Big Growl. But she is so fast, and clever—and ruthless. She became Beta *very* quickly!"

"That's . . . impressive," said Lucky, feeling a strange twist of pain deep in his belly.

"Enough," said Twitch, putting his paws up against a tree and sniffing thoroughly at a hole in the trunk. "It's *really* important we check the boundary just the way Moon would, or she'll have something to say to us about it later."

Lucky cocked his head thoughtfully. *But how would Moon know if you had done your job well or not? Is she really so terrifying that you think she can see you from back at the camp? You are so afraid of Moon and Fiery and Alpha—and Sweet—you don't dare do anything even the tiniest bit different. . . .*

The tree shadows had shortened since they had set out. Lucky followed carefully in Dart's and Twitch's tracks, but as he sniffed and peered, he noticed that they were following *old* paw prints. When the other two stopped to scent-mark, a stale, similar odor was easily detectable in the same place. As his nostrils flared, Lucky tasted the same scents on his tongue, but even older.

They're following the same tracks they follow every day, Lucky thought, astonished. *The same routine, every time. This is crazy!* When Dart glanced up anxiously at the Sun-Dog and yapped, "sun-high," they turned back toward camp as if ordered by an invisible Pack leader.

Now their route took them deeper into the forest, where there were hollows and hillocks and thick scrub to check and double-check, and Lucky had time to think. He doubted that Moon would approve if she knew how slavishly these two followed her old example. Any strange dog who watched the patrol for two or three Sun-Dog journeys would notice the pattern and know how to avoid it.

Alpha had created a disciplined Pack and provided them with a secure and comfortable home, but perhaps even that had disadvantages. Lucky and Bella and the Leashed Dogs had always been alert, always ready to flee or defend themselves at a moment's notice, simply because they felt so insecure. In contrast, Alpha's Pack felt too safe, *too* confident. They must have been here for a long time, perhaps even since before the Big Growl.

It seemed likely. Twitch and Dart were not on constant lookout for trees crashing down, and there certainly was not the kind of devastation here that there had been in the city—or even farther down the valley. One or two fallen trunks blocked their way, but Twitch and Dart bounded up and over them quite dismissively, taking little notice, and showing no sign of nerves. Perhaps, thought Lucky with a small shiver, this Wild Pack was simply too tough and hardened to be bothered by an occasional shake or snarl from the Earth-Dog? On the other paw, perhaps they simply didn't recognize the danger.

From the top of a rough, sandy ridge, Lucky panted as he pricked his ears and stared across the next bay. Yes, it was as he had thought—if Bella and her Pack kept clear of this jutting tongue of land, and the bay to this side of it, there was a shallow gully that they could slip along unseen. If they kept quiet, and stayed careful, and avoided a windy day when their scent might carry far enough for Alpha's Pack to catch it, he thought they would be able to sneak down to the farther side of the lake, and drink there.

Lucky felt a surge of satisfaction. His friends had a good chance.

"Come on!" yipped Dart imperiously as Lucky hesitated on the ridge.

Reluctantly Lucky followed.

The trees were thinning again as they got closer to the camp. Across a broad green meadow Lucky could see the dense, dark line of another forest, one that seemed even vaster than Alpha's territory. A little way ahead, prey-creatures burst from the grass in a panic, hurtling for deeper cover as they scented the dogs, and Lucky's heart leaped with the thrill of the hunt. Almost at his feet, a small shadow flickered in the grass, and Lucky pounced, his paw catching the mouse's tail and pinning it.

He was about to bark his success to the others when he felt a weight slam into his side, knocking him onto his flank. As he hit the ground, Lucky saw the terrified mouse scuttle and vanish, and he stared after it in disbelief. Then he rolled to his feet, hackles up, and glared at Dart.

"Why did you do that? I had it!"

"You had no business having it!" snapped Dart.

Twitch hobbled up. "We do not hunt," he said sharply. "Not on patrol."

Lucky panted in disbelief. "What are you talking about? Why would you not hunt when food walks right in front of you?"

"Maybe you hunt alone in the city," said Dart scornfully. "But *we* are a Pack, and the Pack tells us when to hunt. And that will be when we have earned our place as hunters!"

"Your place?" Lucky yelped, unable to believe what he was hearing. These dogs seemed . . . *trained.* "All dogs hunt! It's *natural.*"

"Not patrol dogs. If we get promoted to the hunting den, it will be because we have earned it. Hunting is not our job, and it is not our right, either."

Lucky looked from one to the other. They stared at him with such disapproval, he could not help his head dropping. "But I was not going to eat it straight away. I was—"

"The hunters will come out later," Twitch told him. "Fiery will lead them out just as the Sun-Dog starts to yawn. That way the patrols are back in camp to support Alpha and guard Moon,

119

and the food is brought back to camp to be shared at no-sun." As Lucky opened his jaws to object, he snapped, "That's how it works! Don't bring your city ways to *our* Pack, Lucky."

Lucky scratched fiercely at one ear, then shook himself and followed the other two obediently, with just one longing look after a last fleeing mouse. He supposed it was natural that the Pack would wish to defend their food source, and ensure that all the food was shared equally by all. If dogs hunted individually— like that nameless one who had eaten the rabbit—they might be tempted to take more than their share.

Oh, Forest-Dog, he thought dismally, *I have so much to learn about Wild Pack life. Don't let me make another mistake like that. . . .*

He could not help a heavy sense of sadness in his gut, though. Twitch and Dart had been perfectly content to let all that prey elude them, which meant that there had to be a *lot* of food in this territory. Yet Bella and her Pack were farther up the valley, desperately hungry and unsure how long they could survive without taking serious risks, like stealing from the Wild Pack. If Alpha had been willing to share, there would be more than enough for all the dogs. It seemed such a waste, and so unfair.

There was no point in Lucky suggesting such a thing, though. One word in favor of the Leashed Dogs, and his new Packmates would be instantly suspicious.

And Lucky had a feeling that Alpha would need no more than a twinge of doubt to throw him out of the Pack, or worse. *Do not let them get the faintest scent of what you really are, Lucky,* he told himself.

He was treading on the shakiest of river-stones. He did not want to fall and be swept away—and become just another dog the Pack was afraid to name.

CHAPTER ELEVEN

By the time the Moon-Dog was stretching lazily on the horizon, Lucky was regretting the loss of the mouse more than he'd thought possible. Hunger bit at his stomach. He lay with his head on his paws, licking his chops and trying not to seem impatient in front of the others. At least, from what Twitch had said, the Pack did *share* the prey that the hunters would bring.

Finally, the hunters returned. The other dogs in the Pack rose to greet them, ears pricked and jaws wet with eagerness, and Lucky took the chance to glance around the camp.

Yes, all the dogs were here—all the ones he knew about, at least. Only Moon was out of sight. She had to be with her pups in their cozy nest. With the whole Pack waiting eagerly for food, this would be a perfect time each day for Bella and the Leashed Dogs to creep down unseen to the lake's far shore. As the undergrowth rustled with the sound of returning dogs, Lucky stored away the knowledge for later, feeling pleased with himself.

Bella's plan might actually work.

The big brown dog—Fiery—advanced into the center of the clearing and dropped a small corpse of prey. He turned his head, sniffing the air, proudly howling to Moon: "We have mice and voles, rabbits and gophers." *And a fat game bird,* Lucky thought, his mouth watering. *And a couple of squirrels. Not a bad share for each of us.*

Spring dropped her catch onto the pile, growling at the broken body of a rabbit. "That one was slippery," she panted. "It almost got away."

Snap gave her ear an affectionate lick. "But you caught it in the end!" Lucky noticed the little dog's fur was stained with mud and blood.

The hunters joined their friends, sitting down to relax. Spring trotted over proudly to Twitch, her head high, and began telling him about the hunt as the limping dog listened appreciatively, his eyes wide with admiration. Mulch and Dart began to tussle, the long-eared black dog rolling the brown-and-white smaller dog over in the dirt as she snapped irritably at his paws. Lucky's stomach growled. He was so *hungry.*

At last, Alpha stalked forward, sniffing approvingly at the prey, and Lucky rose and started eagerly toward the gophers.

He swallowed a yelp when he felt a hard nip on his flank, and turned to see Dart baring her teeth in a warning.

"Not yet!" she growled in a low voice.

Mistake! None of the others had made a move, so Lucky quickly backed down and lay beside Dart and Twitch. "Sorry," he murmured. "Does Alpha divide the food himself?"

They watched as Alpha selected the plump bird along with the best of the rabbits, and settled himself down to pluck and tear at the prey with his teeth.

Lucky glanced around at the other dogs, but none of them had moved at all. They either lay with their heads on their paws, or sat patiently, with their tails flicking the grass, while Alpha ate his fill. On the other side of the circle, Fiery was deep in conversation with Sweet.

Lucky's stomach rumbled. "I don't understand," he said. "Don't we all get to eat?"

"One at a time," said Dart, her eyes glimmering in amusement. "Who in the name of the Moon-Dog taught you manners?"

"It was different in the city," Lucky grumbled.

"We have *rules* here," said Mulch, his nose tilted arrogantly. "We're not greedy scavengers."

Lucky decided not to answer. He had a feeling that, whatever he said, Mulch would scoff.

Alpha was taking his time, cracking the bones with his jaws and licking them clean of meat and marrow. Only when he had filled his belly, stretched, and padded away did Sweet step forward; and only when she had eaten a gopher and two whole voles did Fiery approach the prey. The huge dog tossed a whole squirrel toward the cowering Omega, who barked a humble "Thank you" before taking it away toward Moon's nest in the undergrowth.

Drool slowly fell from the little dog's jaws, but Omega didn't even dare lick at the prey in his mouth. He dropped it at Moon's paws. Lucky realized Omega thanked Fiery for nothing more than the "privilege" of taking Moon's food to her. As he watched three squirming pup noses sniff curiously at the meat even though they weren't old enough to eat it, Lucky pondered how odd the rules of Pack life were.

Could I ever get used to living like this?

Lucky's dismay mounted as he watched the heap of food shrink. The game bird was gone, as were all but one of the rabbits. There were far fewer mice, too. *What's going to be left for me?* He had never really considered it before, but now he keenly felt how rotten it was to be bottom of the Pack.

Fiery was still gobbling down a gopher, licking his red muzzle before tearing into its rib cage again. Lucky's tormented stomach was growling like an angry Alpha, so he almost missed the slinking shadow off to his left. Then he started, and turned.

Mulch was creeping through the twilight shadows, targeting a mouse that had fallen away from the main pile. His paw reached out, almost as if he was only stretching his muscles. . . .

But Lucky wasn't the only one who had noticed Mulch. As one of his claws caught the mouse's tail, Sweet lunged for him, biting his long black ear savagely. Mulch dropped the mouse with a yelp.

"What do you think you're doing?" snapped Sweet. "Stay back until it's your turn! One more trick like that and you will be demoted."

Mulch whimpered an apology, scuttling backward as blood dripped from his torn ear. Lucky felt his heart sink inside him. What had happened to the shy, gentle Sweet he'd known in the Trap House?

"Snap," the swift-dog announced. "Hurry up, or we'll be here until the Moon-Dog goes to sleep."

"Coming, Beta!"

Sweet's new aggression wasn't all that dismayed Lucky. What would remain of the night's hunt for the dogs who held the lower statuses? There wasn't much left in the way of gophers now, and the remaining squirrels were all scrawny. Once Snap had taken her share, it was Mulch's proper turn. Subdued, the black dog snatched up a mouse and a squirrel's leg and scurried back, as if afraid of more punishment.

"Go on, Spring." Sweet broke off her conversation with Fiery to snap another command.

Spring, the hunt-dog who looked so like Twitch, stepped up hungrily and began to feed as Lucky glanced at Twitch.

"Is she your litter-sister?" he asked.

Twitch nodded. "Of course, *she* wasn't born with a useless paw," he growled, holding up his own. "But that's luck for you. That's why she's higher than me in the Pack."

Lucky tried not to let his sympathy show; he had a feeling Twitch wouldn't thank him for it. "But Pack status can change, can't it? You could move up in the ranks?"

"Yes, and you can move *down*," Twitch pointed out gruffly.

Lucky licked his lips nervously, watching the dwindling mound of prey now, sensing tingles in his flanks that felt oddly close to dread. "How does it work? I mean, how does Alpha decide?"

"Alpha and Beta, you mean," Twitch grumbled. "She advises him a lot. There are all kinds of ways to change your Pack-place.

If you do something stupid or wicked or rash—something that puts the Pack in danger—you will be demoted. Do something really stupid or rebellious, and you'll be lucky if demotion is all that happens to you. But if you do well, or serve the Pack, you will rise. That can take a long time, though." He sighed, ears drooping. "It always seems to be a lot easier to fall down than it is to climb up."

Lucky could imagine that. "Can a dog *ask* to be promoted?"

"Of course. But that involves challenging one of your Pack-mates to a fight. That's why I'm stuck where I am. I've tried a few combats . . ." Twitch glared resentfully at his lame paw. "But I never win. The only dog I could beat in a fight is Omega, and who couldn't? I'm just glad he's around to do all the dirty work. Oh, good! Dart has finished. My turn, finally."

Twitch limped forward to the diminished food-heap and began to eat the scrawnier of the squirrels and a leftover piece of rabbit. Waiting his turn, Lucky stole a glance at the miserable Omega, who stood on the very fringe of the Pack, shivering— from the cold, or hunger, Lucky could not quite tell. He felt sorry for the wretched dog, but at the same time deeply grateful there was a dog lower than he was in this Pack. Guilty as it made him, he could understand Twitch's feelings completely.

His thoughts wandered back to his own friends. Who would have been the Omega Leashed Dog, if Bella had run her Pack by these rules? Not Daisy; she was too spirited. . . . Sunshine? He shivered to think of poor Sunshine being treated this way, with her hopelessness at living in the wild, and her obsession with her silky fur. Or maybe it would have been little Alfie?

If Alpha hadn't killed him.

When Twitch had finished and Lucky padded forward, he felt a huge rush of relief. There was most of a gopher left for him, along with a half-chewed haunch of squirrel. It was no kind of feast, but it would be enough to satisfy his gnawing hunger. And for Omega, there would still be . . .

A scrawny shrew.

Lucky stared at it, his stomach burning with guilt. Catching Omega's mournful eyes as he cracked the rabbit's thigh bone, he pushed aside a detached foreleg with his paw, shoving it surreptitiously closer to the dead shrew. He could manage without that mouthful, whereas Omega . . .

Teeth snapped harshly, right against his ear. Lucky flinched, nearly dropping the rabbit leg.

"Next time, I will bite it off," growled Sweet in the silence.

Lucky gazed up at her, dumbstruck. "But—"

"No pity in this Pack, do you hear me? Fill your belly. You are a patrol dog, and I will rip your ear off if you let us down because of weakness. Eat your fill or leave this Pack right now. Do you understand?"

The eyes of every Pack member were on him. Lucky heard murmurs from some of the dogs, who seemed unable to believe what had happened. He heard Mulch growl, "That must be his City-Dog ways."

Desperately Lucky searched Sweet's face, looking for some trace of fellow-feeling, some hint that this display was only for the Pack's benefit. But her gaze was unforgiving. She wasn't doing this for show; she meant it.

So this was how she'd risen so far and so fast in the Pack. There was a ruthlessness in his friend that Lucky had not seen when they were captives in the Trap House, and she had clearly learned to use it.

"Your pity won't do Omega any favors," said Sweet, with a disdainful glance at the ugly little animal.

"I know. I just—"

"It seems that you need a lesson in Pack life, *City Dog.*"

There were muffled sniggers from some of the other dogs at Sweet's words, and Mulch in particular seemed to be enjoying his humiliation—probably because it took the focus away from his own bad behavior. "Indulge this pathetic dog's weakness—pamper him with food he has not earned—and he will never rise any higher in the Pack. Will he?"

Alpha watched her approvingly, and Lucky felt his belly burn with jealousy as well as shame. "I understand . . . Beta," he said.

"Good. If you do not give him a reason to, he will never better himself. Will you, Omega?"

The little dog snuffled and nodded, submissive. "Yes, Beta. You are right." He gave Lucky a resentful glare. "I don't want your pity."

Alpha gave a growling laugh. "Well said, for once, Omega. The City Dog would be holding you under his paw, not helping you." When the dog-wolf's unsettling eyes turned on him, Lucky found himself cowering inwardly. "You are not yet fully *accepted* in this Pack, Lucky. It would be wise of you to remember this—and do things our way from now on."

Sweet gazed at Lucky, her anger replaced with a sort of thoughtfulness. "He will learn, Alpha. I guarantee it."

With those words, Lucky's telling-off seemed to be over. He was grateful to Sweet for bringing it to a close. As he settled back to his food, subdued, he felt a reluctant admiration for her. Deep inside him—right there in his dog-spirit—he understood she was right. Sweet was not simply being harsh; she was being fair, and true to the Pack. Omega would not be allowed to starve, after all—the Pack needed him too much for all the lowly jobs. And Lucky sensed the Forest-Dog would approve of Sweet's savage discipline, the spur that would make Omega try harder to improve his rank.

All the same, none of that made Lucky feel any better. His appetite gone, he turned back to his rabbit and tore at it without enthusiasm, gulping down meat that tasted bitter.

"Wonder how much he'll leave for Omega now," he heard Mulch say.

"It's his first meal with us," said Snap, her voice low and even. "I'm sure he'll learn our ways soon."

Lucky swallowed another mouthful of tough meat, wondering at how this Pack of dogs could work so well together in some ways, even as they seemed to have regular disagreements. Snap wasn't exactly standing up for him, but she was still quick to tell Mulch he was wrong. And yet, there was a sense that everyone was pulling in the same direction, hoping to achieve the same goals.

Packs are just strange, I suppose, he told himself, thinking about

Bella and the Leashed Dogs. They may have been clumsy hunt-ers who pined pathetically for the security of their lives with the longpaws, but none of them would have willingly seen a Packmate go hungry. This Wild Pack, on the other hand, were content to talk lazily among themselves as they watched Omega creep forward to nibble on his scraps, stretching out his time with the shrew to make it last longer, chewing down even the tiny bones.

Neither Pack was where Lucky belonged. More than ever he wished he could be on his own again, free and easy, with respon-sibilities to no one: no dog to lord it over him, and none that he could bully and boss himself. He could barely stand to watch as Omega bit hungrily at the last bare bones.

The Pack dogs were stretching now, getting to their feet, shaking themselves, and licking the last traces of blood from their chops. Almost before Omega had gulped his last sliver, they were gathering in a new circle, away from the prey-tree, and Twitch whined to beckon Lucky over.

He was rising to join them when a new sound swelled around the clearing. Lucky's breath caught in his throat and he paused, his misery forgotten as he listened. The sound seemed to echo in the marrow of his bones before it broke on the air. He raised his head, a thrill lifting his fur.

The Pack had turned their eyes to the darkened sky. The noise that came from their throats was high and wild and haunting. As Lucky stared, he caught sight of Omega's small shadow slipping past him. Two of the dogs in the circle made way for him and the little creature took his place between them, lifting his muzzle and singing out a long howl to the stars.

Shivering, Lucky crept forward. Just as it had for Omega, a space opened for him in the circle, and he found himself next to Sweet, her slender head aimed toward the sky as she howled.

For a moment she grew quiet, pricking her ears to hear the song of the Pack, and she turned her head to Lucky, her eyes distant and solemn. There was no trace now of the arrogant Beta dog.

"At night we howl to the Spirit Dogs," Sweet told him softly. "Sing with us, Lucky. Join the Great Howl."

Those words were like a spirit-force inside him, filling his bones and guts and muscles—something mystical that had to be released into the air, into the sky . . . into the world. His spine tingled with an unfamiliar longing, a need. Lucky tilted his head to the night and howled with the other dogs.

On the opposite side of the circle he saw the black-and-white shape of Moon joining the circle, and the round, fat shadows of her three pups. Even they, with their half-blind eyes, opened their tiny, soft jaws and whimpered little cries to the sky. Though he had never had a glimpse of them beyond their noses before, a surge of fierce pride and protectiveness filled Lucky's body and he howled longer and louder: for the Pack's pups, for Omega, for Sweet and Alpha and the rest.

The stars seemed to whirl above him, breaking and reforming into the shapes of running dogs. Not just the stars, though: As if imprinted on the inside of his eyes he saw other dogs, shadow-dogs, flickering across his mind. The ghostly silhouette of a great hound raced between the slender pine trunks of a huge forest; another tumbled through a surging river, but not drowning or fighting: It was part of the torrent, swift and joyful. Clouds drifted across a bright sky, and between them leaped slender, ferocious Warrior-Dogs, springing from cloud to cloud, their leader a bright slash of light that hurt the eyes.

In his very bones, Lucky was aware that the dogs around him were howling to particular Spirit Dogs. There was a high, silvery note to Moon's howling that her pups did their tiny best to echo; Lucky wondered if she was crying out *only* to the Moon-Dog. Dart, the brown-and-white patrol dog, let out a cry to the Sky-Dogs, so fierce and clear that it somehow seemed to echo as far as the horizon. Fiery's deep rumbling howl was as rich as rocks and soil; and though Mulch's cry was thinner, it too was filled with love of the landscape. The two of them were calling, each in his own way, to the Earth-Dog.

And the Spirit Dogs answered them.

Was he imagining the phantom hounds that raced across his vision? Lucky hesitated, opening an eye and breaking the spell for a fleeting instant. Were the other Pack members seeing them, too? It was impossible to tell. Closing his eyes, he resumed his howling, higher and fiercer than before, and he thought he heard an answering song within him: the great ghostly dog that hunted through the dream-trees in his mind's eye.

Lucky felt like he could howl forever. The Spirit Dogs were inside him—they were inside all of them, joining with the Pack and leaping in the shadows around them.

But slowly, gradually, the Great Howl died away as the ghostly dogs faded from his vision. Lucky wasn't quite sure when the last faint howl was swallowed up by the night and the silence fell, but he blinked as if he had awoken from a dream—a dream he did not want to end. The surge of loyalty still tingled in his flesh, and he felt a huge, irresistible tug toward every member of

the Pack. He forgot his feelings of only moments ago: his resentment, his shame and humiliation. These were his brothers, his
sisters, his hunting-and-fighting friends, and he would never
leave them, never. . . .

It was fleeting, fading, but the intensity of that Pack-spirit
lingered in his brain and heart. Now he saw what bound these
dogs together, despite the brutality and harshness of their lives.
For the first time, he could truly understand what Sweet had
told him.

Lucky felt dizzy with the echo of the Great Howl as he padded
silently to the patrol den, where Dart and Twitch were already
yawning and treading their ritual circles. The leaf-strewn space
was close to the entrance of the clearing, and Lucky knew that no
enemy could get past them, not with Twitch and Dart on guard
there with their ears pricked and their eyes shining. A fierce certainty raced through him: No dog would get past him to his leader,
to his Pack and the Pack's pups. No dog would dare. . . .

As he lay down, his head on his paws and his ears still alert
for any threat, he gazed at the softest hollow of all—the sheltered
glade that was Alpha's sleeping place. The dog-wolf was curled
up there with Sweet, his massive tail tucked close to her slender
muzzle.

Something other than loyalty and protectiveness was shivering through Lucky's flesh now. It was not Pack-love that prickled his neck and raised his hackles . . .

It was the sharp fang bite of jealousy.

CHAPTER TWELVE

Jaws, snapping and tearing . . .

The screaming barks and yelps of wounded dogs . . .

The howls of battle-rage as teeth tore into flesh.

Two shadowy leaders howled their hate at each other, commanding their Packs to rip and kill. . . . And they did, two armies destroying themselves, dragging each other down, down to the Earth-Dog. Sharp fangs sank into Lucky's ear, just as Sweet had threatened that hers would do, and he felt that ear ripped from his skull. But when he spun around to defend himself he could see only darkness, could feel only the spatter of blood in his face. There was no enemy for him to fight, no way of battling to survival.

There was only a raging torrent of savagery. . . .

The Storm of Dogs—

Lucky started awake with a terrified growl. The muzzle that nudged and nipped him was no horrifying phantom. It was just

Twitch. The black-and-tan long-eared dog's weak leg was shaking with weariness as he limped to lie down near Lucky.

"Wake up, Lucky. It's your turn on watch."

Lucky got to his feet, his own legs trembling. He took deep breaths to calm his fear. There was no battle—no dying and killing—only the same forest hollow where he had slept for five no-suns now. The woods were silent around them but for the whisper of branches, and the rustle of beetles and other small prey.

"Go on, Lucky!" Twitch insisted. "I need to sleep."

Stretching, shaking his fur, Lucky let Twitch slump into his sleeping place with a tired sigh. "I haven't been on watch before. Are you sure—"

"Beta says you're ready. She says that you fit in now, and that you show commitment to the Pack." There was approval in Twitch's voice. "She says that she trusts you. That means we *all* do."

Lucky gave a soft growl of acceptance and pleasure. "Where should I patrol? And who will be with me?"

"At night, we patrol alone," Twitch said. "You just have to pad around the edge of the camp, and keep your eyes open for anything that should worry us. Since you'll be by yourself, it's safer to keep moving. Don't stay in one place too long."

Still bleary, and a little shaken by his dream, Lucky made his way to the clearing's entrance. He was tired, but he was grateful as well for being woken from that terrible dream. And he could not deny a glow of pride that Sweet thought him so worthy of trust. He had been with them now for only four full journeys of the Sun-Dog, yet he was being given responsibility for guarding the whole Pack.

He would not let them down.

Just as he was thinking this, his gut turned over with realization. For a moment, in the blurry aftermath of sleep, he had forgotten the real reason he was here. Each night, the Great Howl drew him in and wound its spell tight around his heart, bonding him closer to the Wild Pack. Each morning he woke, remembering the thrill in his blood, and the memory was always followed by a sting of shame and disgust. How easy it was to forget, to be drawn in—to feel his blood singing that he was one of them, a Wild Dog, forever.

But the shame grew less each morning.

No! Again he reminded himself that he was *not* part of this Pack. He was here on a mission, and now was the time for him to fulfill it. He might not have a better moment to slip away, to reveal the Wild Pack's weak points to Bella. And once he was gone, he would not come back. Not ever.

The Wild Dogs might never even know it was him who had betrayed them.

Lucky shook himself violently from head to tail. He shouldn't be feeling this sadness, this crawling regret, in his belly. Twitch and Dart would miss him on patrol. He wondered what they would think had happened to him. At least he wouldn't have to face any of them again. Not even Sweet . . . A sick sensation filled his belly.

He shook it off angrily. He couldn't let Bella and the others down. With a last glance over his shoulder at the silent, sleeping camp, Lucky slunk away into the shadows of the forest.

Good-bye, he told them silently. *I'm sorry that I had to do this to you.*

The Moon-Dog was high overhead as Lucky picked his way cautiously through scrub and tree trunks, and he found himself wondering if Bella would still be at their meeting place. He barely liked to admit what a relief it would be if she had already left. Maybe she had given up on him altogether, after waiting in vain the last few no-suns. He could go on alone . . . or return to the Wild Pack. . . .

As he crept into the great open space, he could smell the

longpaw-place, all old fires and burnt food as Bella had described it. He saw the strange shapes of tables and benches, silvered by the Moon-Dog's light. Beneath one of them, a cracked and over-turned board of nailed planks, he saw curled shadows that moved slightly: flanks that rose and fell with breath.

Bella and Mickey, huddled together and fast asleep. Lucky padded to them on silent paws and licked gently at their faces.

"Bella? Mickey?"

They were awake in an instant, leaping to their feet, hackles high and snarling. Lucky saw the bright glint of their wide eyes.

"It's me. Lucky."

Both Bella and Mickey relaxed, their breaths coming out in a relieved sigh. Tails lashing, they yipped soft greetings, exchanging licks with Lucky. He was so happy to see them again; it felt like an age since he had left his friends to join the Wild Pack. And he was shocked to realize just how much he had missed his litter-sister. Fondly he nuzzled her ear.

"It's good to see you safe," he murmured. "How are Bruno and Martha?"

Bella seemed to hesitate for a moment, but Mickey shook his head and barked gruffly, "Not good. We've given them the best of the food and the cleanest of the water, but they don't seem to be getting any better." The Farm Dog's eyes were downcast, as if he was ashamed to give Lucky such bad news.

Lucky's heart sank. His friends could not be eating or drinking well if there had not been much recovery; he felt bad now for resenting his small share of the Wild Pack's prey. At least he had been able to eat. . . .

Again he felt his loyalties shift, and the guilt gnaw at his belly. "I'm sorry it's taken so long. I did not dare creep away before now. There were always dogs watching."

"We understand. But the poison creeps farther and farther downriver," said Bella quietly. "And the hunting is poor. I suppose the prey is all moving away from the bad water, too. And every time it rains, we have to get out of the caves quickly, in case they flood. I can't afford to have that river water touching anyone else."

"That's sensible." Lucky licked her. "But it must be very difficult."

"Please, Lucky." Bella raised her golden eyes to his. "Please tell me you've found a way for us to get to the lake."

"Yes, I have." Lucky did his best to look cheerful, for Mickey's and Bella's sake. "Listen, the Wild Pack still will not let you share."

"But—"

"No, wait. I've scouted out a way we can get to the lake without them seeing us, and I know the best time as well. There's a gully—I'll show you where it runs—and we need to follow it around the long way to the far side of the lake. The patrols do not go that far, and if it's a still night there won't be enough wind to carry our scent to them. I think it will be safe for us to drink then."

"You think?" Bella looked doubtful, and Mickey gave her a worried glance.

"The best time is sunset," Lucky went on. "Not only is that a good time to travel—because the dusk gives good camouflage—but that is the time the hunters come back to the Pack. The whole Pack eats together, so no dog will be patrolling."

He did not want to mention the Great Howl, though he could not say why this was. Perhaps because the very thought of it gave him that ache of Pack-longing in his belly. . . .

Mickey pawed the ground, and Bella furrowed her brows. "I'm not sure that Bruno and Martha will be strong enough," she said.

"That'll be all right," said Lucky. "We can take all the fit and strong dogs down to the lake, and that should leave enough clean water back at camp for the sick ones. See?"

The Leashed Dogs exchanged a glance—one that he did not like, though he couldn't say why. Mickey shuffled some leaves into a pile with a paw, the pointless task seeming to fascinate him. Bella peered at the stars above her, as if searching intently for the shape of the Rabbit or one of the other star-creatures their mother had pointed out to them when they were just pups.

"I can't tell you how glad I am to be coming back." Lucky's voice was too bright; he could hear it himself. "I've missed you all!"

"Lucky?" With a great sigh, Bella raised her eyes to meet his. "You shouldn't come back . . . not yet."

"What?" He was startled. "But I've found the way—"

"No." Bella shook her head determinedly. "You have done a wonderful job, Lucky, but don't you see? That Wild Pack trusts you now. You can slip away without anyone suspecting anything is wrong. You might be able to find out more! Stay with them a little longer, Lucky—for us."

Lucky stared at her. The thought of going back to the Wild Pack after betraying them like this filled him with shame as well as guilt. And what if they had noticed his absence? He did not like the idea of having to explain himself to Alpha—or to Sweet, who had trusted him to watch over the camp. Would she get in trouble for what he had done?

Yet he did want to see Sweet again. And not just because of what he had to do for Bella and her friends.

I can take part in the Howl again. . . . I can feel the power of the Earth-Dog and the Sky-Dogs. I can feel like I'm in control of myself, my destiny—rather than rushing around, simply trying to stay alive.

His fur bristled with sadness at that thought. Without him, would the Leashed Dogs be *able* to survive? His litter-sister was becoming stronger and more confident—he could see that—but even she seemed not to understand the world around them in the way that the dogs in Alpha's Pack did. They would always need his help.

"All right," he said at last. "I will go back. But, Bella . . ."

"What?" His litter-sister's voice sounded sharp, almost on edge.

Lucky shook himself. "Nothing. I just want you to know I don't like this. *Any* of it."

As he turned and walked away, he was almost sure he caught a guilty look passing between Bella and Mickey, but he shrugged it off. He did not mind if they had to share a little bit of his own unhappiness.

Moon-Dog was already settling down to sleep through the day, and Sun-Dog would soon replace her on the horizon. Lucky felt a fearful urgency to get back to Alpha's camp before they realized he was missing, but he was nervous, too. He stopped every few paces to listen, and to sniff at the breeze. One sign of an early patrol and he would have to take to his paws and run back to Bella. There was no excuse he could think of for abandoning his watch until sunup.

Birds were beginning to sing in the branches above him, and one took off with a flutter of wings. Lucky halted, his heart in his throat, but the bird settled; there was nothing else, no bark, no howl of alarm or anger. His paws shook slightly as he went on. He noticed there was a scent that clung to his coat, and recognized it as Bella's. A shudder went down his spine; how had he imagined the other dogs would not notice that?

He plunged deep into a pile of dead leaves that had rotted almost to mulch, rolling over and over until he was sure he had rid himself of her smell.

Finally he reached the outskirts of the Wild Pack's camp. Unable to suppress the tingle of fear in his skin, he padded silently closer, listening for the stir of dogs waking up.

Silence. Lucky was in his post by the clearing entrance just in time to see Spring stretching and rising, yawning at the morning, her long brown-and-black ears dangling, her keen nose twitching as she picked up the scents all around them. Lucky tilted his head and watched her expectantly as she trotted up and licked his ear.

"Any trouble, Lucky?" she asked quietly.

"None," he lied. *Only the trouble I brought myself....*

"Go and get some sleep, then." Spring sat down in his place, her eyes sweeping the forest beyond. "I'll keep my nose out for any danger."

"*Is* there any danger?" Lucky asked.

"Not really," Spring replied. "It would be a foolish dog who tried to take us on."

"I suppose you're right," said Lucky as Spring loped off. He turned his sleep-circle on the patch of soft moss that was his bed, glancing up into the sky and hoping the Sky-Dogs were listening to him.

I am sorry for being such a dishonorable dog, but my friends need help....

He lay down, shutting his eyes, but sleep refused to come. No doubt the Moon-Dog was angry. *Oh, Forest-Dog, please explain to her that I had to do it.*

It was no use. Besides, every time his eyes closed, his terrible nightmare of the Storm of Dogs rumbled distantly, threatening to return. Between the dream and the way his loyalties seemed to bite and scratch at each other, he knew he wouldn't be able to sleep now. But if he was up and wandering the camp after patrolling during the night, other dogs would ask questions. And Lucky felt like he had told enough lies recently.

This was why he had always preferred living as a Lone Dog. Who could bear being torn in so many directions? Loyalty to other dogs was a curse, he thought bitterly, because you could not be loyal to everyone at once. How in the name of the Sky-Dogs had a loner like him come to run with two Packs, and somehow not *belong* to either?

It's like the Big Growl turned the whole world upside down, he thought.

The Sun-Dog was pushing his muzzle above the horizon, a bright glow of gold that lit up the whole forest and burnished the pine bark with shining bronze. There would be no more sleep now, Lucky realized with an inward sigh.

He did not want to lie here anyway. If he did, he knew that thoughts would tumble around his head more and more. How was he going to get himself out of this mess without disappointing— or betraying—dogs that he cared about?

CHAPTER THIRTEEN

"Hold on!" barked Dart. "Everybody stay still!"

Lucky lifted his head and pricked his ears, watching Dart carefully as she sniffed the wind, her fur prickling. Her muzzle was curled back, and Lucky felt a tremor of unease in his flanks.

Sometimes, he got the feeling Dart *hoped* for there to be trouble—so she had something to snarl and fight about. She was an angry dog.

The sunup patrol had been straightforward, thank the Sky-Dogs, because Lucky knew he was too tired and confused to deal with any nasty surprises. But what could Dart have noticed in this broad, pleasant meadow, with a clear view of any possible danger from far away? All Lucky could see was rippling grass, right up to the dark line of forest beyond.

"What is it?" he howled.

"I don't know." Dart sniffed the air again, urgently. "Something strange."

Twitch was silent too, casting around for any scent of what Dart had detected. Lucky followed Twitch as he drew closer to Dart; he hoped that what Dart had found had nothing to do with Bella's Pack. He wasn't sure he trusted Bella not to do something stupid without him there to talk her out of it. What if they had strayed into Alpha's territory in their desperate search for food?

Suddenly Lucky stopped, one paw raised. He was close to Dart now and a hint of the strange scent had come to him, too. It took him only a second to identify it: crushed earth, metal, and animal-hide . . . That strong-smelling drink that a longpaw would give to a . . .

Loudcage!

It was no ordinary loudcage, though; it was one of those monstrous ones he would occasionally see in the city. They smelled different from the little loudcages—stronger and more threatening. Lucky had seen them chew up entire roads, spitting out black chunks of earth and flattening them beneath terrible crushing feet that rolled across the earth.

"Stop, Dart—I know what that is!"

Dart threw him a doubtful look, then slunk across to Lucky. "What?" she muttered.

"It's a loudcage scent, but that's a *big* one—"

Dart flinched away, a spark of terror in her eyes. "Loud-cages? Well, they have nothing to do with us. Let's go on with the patrol—avoid the thing—"

"They won't threaten us, not those ones with the great teeth," Lucky told her. "They are too big to bother with us. We should go and see what they are up to."

"No," Dart growled. "Why should we care that loudcages are nearby?"

"Because they can crush a dog," Lucky told them. "Not even the fastest dog can outrun a loudcage."

"Maybe Beta could," said Twitch, who had come to stand with them. "She's very fast."

"Not even her," Lucky whined. "We must be careful now."

"I've never seen a loudcage," Twitch said, his flanks heaving as he shivered. "I've never even heard of such a thing as a giant one."

"Of course not," snapped Dart, who seemed very much on edge. "You and Spring were born in the wild. I lived in the city when I was a pup, and I've *seen* the terrible things a loudcage can do. One of my littermates . . ." She shuddered.

Maybe Dart was right, thought Lucky. Maybe they should avoid the giant loudcage. But what was it doing out here in the wild? Were the longpaws building a new city to replace their destroyed one? If that was so, it was surely better for the dogs to know about it, so that they could move on in plenty of time.

"Just a quick look," Lucky promised. "I'm sure Alpha would want us to investigate."

That was enough to persuade the other two. Hesitantly they followed Lucky as he tracked the scent—which was not difficult when the smell of loudcage drink was so thick and overwhelming. Lucky felt quite sick with it by the time they crested a rise and saw a marshy plain stretching out below.

There it was: a colossal yellow loudcage, resting from its brutal churning of the ground. The tracks of its rolling paws were everywhere, mounds of muddy earth strewn around them. There was another beast with it, a long-snouted metal thing that was driven half into the earth as if hunting for the Earth-Dog herself. Lucky shuddered at the sight.

There were longpaws there, of course, wearing that strange shiny, yellow fur Lucky had seen before on the ones beside the poisoned river.

"Keep back," he growled to Twitch and Dart, but it was hardly necessary. They were already cowering against the fringe of trees. "Those longpaws aren't friendly. You were right, Dart—whatever they're doing, it is not good for us."

But this time it was Twitch who held his ground, staring out from the cover of the long grass. "Look at that giant metal tooth," he whispered. "They are *eating* the ground. Chasing the Earth-Dog. Do you think they're hurting her?"

"If Earth-Dog was hurt," said Dart, "she would let us know. She would Growl again."

"What if they've killed her?" Twitch whined.

"I don't know," snapped Dart, "but Lucky's right. We should leave now."

"No. We said we would find out more and report to Alpha. We have a duty to the Pack."

Twitch had a stubborn, determined look in his eyes. Lucky sighed, annoyed and impatient. Maybe the slower-moving dog was desperate to impress Alpha and improve his standing in the Pack. There was little chance of that, so far as Lucky could see: Speed and strength were what mattered for the higher-ranked hunting dogs, and even Mulch and Spring, who were less experienced and skilled than Fiery or Snap, had nothing to fear from Twitch. But Twitch had a point. The business with the giant loud-cage was strange behavior, even for longpaws—it might be good for the dogs to find out what they were up to.

For the time being, they did not seem to be up to much at

all. The giant loudcage rested, still and silent, while the long-paws ambled around, exchanging curt sounds and inspecting the churned earth. One of them held a box in his hand that seemed very important to him, because he kept touching it, staring at it. Lucky pricked one ear.

It was all they seemed to do—stand and talk and prod the ground, and occasionally peer at the box. Just as Lucky was beginning to think there was nothing more to be learned, one of the longpaws strode up to the giant loudcage and mounted it. After a moment of silence, the loudcage roared—a terrifying sound that made the ground tremble beneath his paws.

With a whine, Lucky crouched low, seeing that Twitch and Dart were doing the same. What were the longpaws doing—trying to provoke another Big Growl? The giant loudcage's roar was constant and deafening, blotting out every other sound in the world. The smell of broken wet earth and disturbed crawling creatures obliterated every other scent. Lucky hated the fact that all his senses could detect was that loudcage and its work.

"We need to get away," he barked at the others. "We're blind and deaf here!"

"Yes!" yelped Twitch. Dart was already scuttling back, her eyes alight with terror.

The sunlight that spilled over them vanished, as if a cloud had drifted across the Sun-Dog. His senses were so confused and blunted, Lucky thought he was imagining it—that the sudden cool dimness was in his head. Then he realized: a shadow cast by . . .

He spun around. A longpaw was behind him, and advancing!

Lucky's neck fur rose up and he barked as loudly as he could, but the longpaw did not hesitate the way he had known some city longpaws do in the face of a strange dog. Dart and Twitch were barking too, teeth bared and ears flattened like Lucky's, but there were more longpaws now. Friends of the ones with the giant loud-cage? They were dressed just the same, though they'd come from the opposite direction. Their faces were black, and seemingly without eyes, noses, or mouths. They wore those yellow, shiny furs.

Worse, each one carried a sharp metal stick.

The back of Lucky's neck prickled almost painfully with the sense of threat. His flesh and fur rippled with fear, as the dogs beside him trembled and snarled. All three dogs let loose another volley of furious barks, but there was no stopping the longpaws.

"Bite them!" shrieked Dart. "Bite!"

"No, we shouldn't do that!" barked Lucky wildly.

"But the sticks! The *sticks!*"

"They'll use the sticks on us if we bite them!" Lucky barked, trying to sound confident. *But they will probably use them anyway!*

Then another sound cut through the air, higher even than the distant roar of the loudcage. This time it was the longpaws who halted, frozen to the spot and looking up in alarm. The sound was a wild, bone-chilling howl, full of menace and death. In that instant, Lucky could smell the longpaws' fear. They reeked of it, even through their shiny yellow fur.

No wonder. Even Lucky felt horror thrill through his guts, and he knew he had nothing to fear—not from his own Alpha. . . .

Everything around them was still; even the loudcage had fallen silent. A few leaves drifted in the breeze, touching a longpaw's eyeless face. The howl came again, echoing eerily, and the longpaws looked all around now, turning, searching desperately for the source of that threatening sound. One of them yelped in unease, but Lucky could not tell which one.

The longpaws were confused and uncertain. It was the dogs' only chance. . . .

"Now!" barked Lucky.

The three of them bolted, skidding past the frozen longpaws and racing for the forest. Lucky heard the longpaws' barks, but he did not look back. He was certain they wouldn't chase them into the trees—not now they'd heard that dreadful menacing howl.

Slowing down once they were under the cover of the trees, with Twitch and Dart at his paws, Lucky drew breath, his heart pounding. Dart was panting with the remnants of panic, but Twitch managed to gasp, "Good for Alpha. That showed them!"

It did, thought Lucky, impressed despite himself. He glanced around, peering through the trees, but he could not see his leader. Nor could he see the longpaws—Alpha's howls had terrified them into submission, and they had not even laid eyes on him.

Delight in their escape, and admiration for his new leader, faded to something far less pleasant as the three dogs made their way carefully back through the unfamiliar patch of woodland. By the time they could smell their own camp again, there was a hot, clenching ball of dread in Lucky's belly.

Who would ever want to get on the wrong side of that lethal, ill-tempered dog-wolf? What dog in his right mind would deliberately set out to deceive and betray Alpha?

Yet, that was *exactly* what Lucky had done.

CHAPTER FOURTEEN

Lucky could feel cold tremors in his skin. Alpha's yellow eyes seemed to focus just on him as the three dogs padded into the clearing, and the tip of the dog-wolf's tail twitched slightly.

What had the dog-wolf known? Lucky wondered. Had his howl been simply a coincidence, or had he saved them deliberately?

Lucky felt the hard tug of tiredness in his bones. He would have liked nothing more than to slump down in his sleeping-place and doze until sun-high, but he knew they had to report to their leader.

"Well?" drawled Alpha, his throat rumbling. "What happened?"

Dart was still out of breath, as much from fear as from the run. "Longpaws, Alpha. And the biggest loudcage I've ever seen."

"Loudcages?" came Fiery's voice. Lucky could not tell if the muscular dog was afraid, or contemplating hunting the enemy.

"It was like a house that could run," Dart continued, and Lucky saw Twitch glance quickly at Spring, the wild-born litter-mates clearly wondering what *house* meant. "Lucky knew what it was."

Alpha turned back to Lucky. "Did he now? Oh, *I* know about loudcages, too. Dirty, dangerous brutes."

"I used to see these big loudcages in the city, Alpha," said Lucky, keeping his eyes low and his tone respectful. "They are not like ordinary loudcages—they can chew up the earth and eat it for dinner. And something else was there, too—"

"What?" Alpha's tongue lashed his jaws.

"I'm not sure. It wasn't another loudcage. It was more like a giant fang, biting into the earth."

"That's right, Alpha," confirmed Dart. "And the longpaws there were like nothing I've ever seen."

"I've seen these longpaws before," said Lucky in a low voice. "They've been around since the Big Growl, lots of them. I think they might have something to do with it."

"They had shiny yellow fur." Twitch shivered. "Black faces without eyes—or mouths! And they weren't afraid of us, as they should have been. They had big sticks, and tried to capture us." The other dogs glanced at one another with alarm, and Omega's ears flattened with fear. Mulch backed a few steps closer to Fiery, the hair on his hackles rising as he growled low in his throat.

Dart took a step forward, giving a short, sharp whine. "But they *were* afraid of you, Alpha."

"Of course," growled the half wolf. "But you were right to flee. Never get closer to longpaws than you have to. It is good that you found out about them, but . . ." His head slowly turned to Lucky. "It was *careless* to put yourself at risk of capture. Don't do that again."

Lucky bit back a retort, his eyes briefly meeting Sweet's. She stood beside Alpha, with a similarly stern look. Lucky tried to see kindness beneath the expression, but wasn't sure it was there. He sank lower to the ground. "Yes, Alpha."

The dog-wolf gave a great wide yawn that showed every one of his white teeth. "Longpaws like these were always encroaching on wolf territory. Always trying to take over the wild, eating up the earth, and stripping the land of cover and prey. Perhaps they are up to the same tricks here. We need to stay alert."

"Yes, Alpha."

Lucky blinked at his leader. It was just the briefest of glimpses into the world of wolves, but still Alpha's words thrummed in his belly, sparking a hot curiosity. Why, he wondered, had Alpha left the wolves to run with dogs? Was it his choice? Or had he been thrown out, perhaps? He would not have been surprised if the wolves viewed a half dog as weaker, inferior.

But he did not dare ask the Pack leader. Instead he went down on his forelegs and flicked his ears forward. "I don't know how you knew we were in trouble, but your howl gave us our chance to escape. I'm grateful to you." Dart and Twitch bowed onto their forelegs as well, their eyes fixed on their leader.

Alpha did not reply for a moment, nor did he explain his insight. He gazed down coolly at Lucky, his tailtip still lightly drumming the ground.

Then he looked away disdainfully. "That? That was nothing. All I did was open my jaws. That's why I'm Alpha of this Pack, *City Dog*." Behind Lucky, Mulch snorted a scornful half laugh.

Feeling awkward and a little humiliated, Lucky rose and stretched, then shook himself. He would have liked to snap at Alpha, but that would have been foolish. What would it have cost the dog-wolf to simply accept his thanks? He had wanted to show his gratitude, because the longpaw attack and their close escape had shaken him to his core. He'd been polite—deferential, even. Yet all Alpha had shown in return was his arrogance.

Lucky felt like a fool. He couldn't win. Alpha's arrogance

gnawed at his patience, making him feel constantly on edge. Great Howl or no Great Howl, he could not live like this.

Alpha had closed his eyes again, as if entirely uninterested, and his huge body sprawled languidly across the rock. Clearly their audience with him was at an end; Twitch and Dart were already drawing an excited circle of listeners with their tale of the terrifying longpaws and their savage loudcage.

"You would not have believed how big it was!"

"And the noise." Dart shook her head violently. "Like nothing you've ever heard!"

As the dogs in the Pack discussed their new threat, their barks and yelps tumbled over one another like play-fighting puppies.

"What damage can loudcages do?"

"Is there any way we can hurt them?"

"Do they really have longpaws *inside* them?"

Lucky knew that, soon, the questions would come to him. He did not feel much like being the center of attention, so he slunk across the clearing to a warm patch of sunlight beneath a thin birch tree.

Remember this feeling, Lucky—you will not be with this Pack forever!

He would have to use his time wisely from now on. Patrolling was all very well, but he'd been in danger of relaxing too easily into his comfortable Pack role, and that was not why he was here. If he was going to find out everything he could about this Pack and its leader, he was going to have to get himself promoted to hunter.

Head on his paws, he breathed out a sigh as he watched Pack life go on around him. Twitch had stretched out on a grassy bank to catch a lucky ray of Sun-Dog's light, and Dart had trotted across to visit with Moon, sniffing affectionately at the clumsily crawling pups, whose eyes had fully opened now. The largest pup tumbled over to land on top of his sister and Moon patiently pushed him upright again.

"Squirm," Moon said. "Be careful." The female pup wobbled back upright, only to trip over Dart's paws. The brown-and-white swift-dog nosed her affectionately.

Fiery, sprawled alongside Mulch, had just growled a lazy order at Omega, who whined submissively before trotting off obediently.

For the moment Pack life was settled, ordered, stable. Each dog knew his place and accepted it. That might be good for the Pack, but it was not what Lucky needed. He had to *rise*, so that he might gain Alpha's trust, and convince him that the Leashed Dogs were not to be feared or attacked. He did not have time to work his way quietly up the ranks, waiting for some other dog to put a paw wrong and be demoted. A small tremor rippled through his spine. *And if I stay here too long, I might get too settled. I might start thinking of this as my Pack.*

He needed to do what he came here to do. And he needed to do it soon. There was only one other way to change his status. He would have to challenge a higher-ranked dog, and then beat him in combat to take his place.

Lucky swallowed hard. Which Packmate would he challenge?

Fiery was pacing toward the nest where Moon still lay with their pups, and Lucky followed him with his eyes. The huge dog was well fed and powerful, sleek with rippling muscle. There was no way he could take on Fiery and win.

Mulch? he wondered. Lucky cocked an ear, thinking hard. He thought he could defeat Mulch . . . but the long-eared black dog's initial dislike of Lucky hadn't lessened, judging by the way he seemed keen on disagreeing with him all the time. He would take a challenge very personally, and very seriously, and would not easily let himself be beaten by a "City Dog." Lucky suspected he would fight dirty if he had to. *And the last thing I need right now is a bad wound.*

Across the clearing, the young tan-and-white Snap basked

in her sleeping-place, her paws and belly turned to the thin rays of light from the Sun-Dog. She was a hunter who ranked above Mulch, Lucky remembered, but she did not have the same vicious resentment. She would not fight so bitterly, and would be less likely to hurt him badly if she defeated him.

Plus, she was smaller than he was. . . .

If I gnaw this over any longer in my head, I'll never do it. Lucky rose and stretched carefully, clawing the mossy ground, testing his muscles. There were no aches that were bothering him. Standing up straight, he shook himself, then padded determinedly to Sweet.

She sniffed at him. "What is it, Lucky?"

He dipped his head slightly in a gesture of respect. "I want to make a challenge, Beta."

Sweet sat back on her haunches. Raising an elegant hind leg she scratched long and painstakingly at her ear, then sat still again, studying his eyes. "Very well," she said crisply. "Who do you wish to fight?"

"Snap," Lucky told her.

There was a hint of an amused gleam in Sweet's soft eyes.

"Good luck," she said with a huffing laugh, and she stood on all four paws and surveyed the clearing. "Packmates! Hear me!"

167

Surprise and curiosity showed in the dogs' faces as they hushed and turned to face her. Ears pricked and tails thumped expectantly.

"Lucky the City Dog challenges Snap the hunter," announced Sweet simply.

Snap's eyes widened as she rolled onto her front. "He does?"

Lucky padded forward from Sweet's side, and dipped his head politely toward Snap.

She gave a small, sharp bark. "You're in a hurry to challenge, new dog."

Is it that obvious? Lucky wondered, as he heard an amused whine on the other side of the camp. "The City Dog must be tired of living." It was Mulch.

Lucky ignored him and gave Snap a gruff bark. "I want to rise in this Pack. I may as well start now."

Snap's reply was a silky growl. "You won't rise too far. But every dog is free to try."

Glancing back, Lucky saw nothing in Alpha's eyes but cynical amusement. Alpha was so far above the others, Lucky realized, their petty challenges meant nothing to him—except perhaps as entertainment.

"Fight me, then." Snap rose and stood squarely before Lucky, her muscles tight as drawn-back branches, white teeth bared.

Her eyes were bright and hard and unafraid, Lucky realized, wondering if he'd bitten off more than he could gnaw. But it was too late to turn back now, and besides, it was a risk he was always going to have to take. He curled back his own muzzle as his hackles stiffened.

Sweet stepped forward, her tail high and her muzzle raised. "Before we begin, do you both understand the consequences? That if Lucky wins, he will join the hunters in Snap's place?"

Lucky said, "Yes," at the same time that Snap growled, "It will not happen!"

"May the Sky-Dogs look with blessing on your combat!" Sweet barked formally. "May your fight be fair, and may the outcome be favored by the Spirit Dogs. When the battle is done, we all remain Packmates. And we all shall protect the Pack!"

Just when Lucky thought Sweet's proclamation might go on forever, the swift-dog closed her muzzle. *Thank the Sky-Dogs there was nothing more for her to say,* he thought. *I'm nervous enough as it is!*

"On my word." Sweet sat down, studying each dog for a long moment. "Now—fight!"

They sprang, claws raking for each other's weak spots: noses, ears, eyes. Snap was a tan-and-white blur, moving quickly, her ears perked forward and her tail curling over her back. She cannoned into Lucky, slamming the breath from his body, and making them roll over and over. She was trying to beat him with shock before they even started, he thought, but that wasn't going to work. Springing back to his paws, he flung her off and circled her warily.

Snap too was upright again, but now she was more cautious. Lucky was a good bit bigger, and as his paws found a slight rise in the ground he took advantage, pouncing from above, teeth gnashing at her tail.

"Watch out for his dirty city tactics, Snap!" Mulch barked.

Snap was fast, though. She yelped and wriggled from beneath Lucky, aiming a snap of her jaws at his flank. He dodged just in time, feeling them scrape along his fur and skin. Snap rolled and leaped back, then darted swiftly under his belly for another nip. An excited yelping rose from the crowd of dogs around them. "Nicely done, Snap!" Fiery barked in approval.

Snarling, Lucky lunged, driving her off, then hopped back a couple of paces. Snap was quick, and had surprisingly strong jaws. She was a trickier opponent than he had expected her to be—but as he'd predicted, she did not have the viciousness of Mulch.

She fought not to hurt or maim her opponent. She fought only for the victory.

Still, Lucky knew she would sink her teeth into his flesh if she needed to.

He growled, slinking sideways to keep her in his sight. This time, when she shot forward for another quick strike, he had time to dodge and lunge for her, grabbing her by the scruff of her neck and shaking hard before releasing her. Snap scuttled out of reach again, panting and snarling. An excited yapping came from the pups. "So fast, Mama!" one said, and Lucky heard Moon give a low bark of agreement.

"Do you give up, City Dog?" Even as Snap caught her breath she was grinning, tongue lolling. "You might be big, but you're very naive."

"Finish him off!" Mulch again, sounding like he wished he were in the fight himself.

Lucky glared a warning at Snap as he stalked, drool dripping from his own jaws. Once again she was quick as Lightning's fire, shooting under him to bite at his hind leg. The move was one he had never seen in the city, and the pain was sharp and hot. Lucky yelped—as much in anger as in pain—and twisted to lash his jaws, catching her ear between his teeth. Snap squealed, but he did not let go, rolling her over with his sheer weight.

Lucky heard a growl of protest from Fiery. "Don't let him take you down, Snap!"

"Release!" Snap screamed as blood began flowing from her ear. "Release!"

"Release," commanded Sweet, and reluctantly Lucky loosened his jaw. It might have been a dirty trick to hang on to Snap's tender ear flesh, but he was a City Dog—as they never tired of telling him—and he would do what he needed to do to get his victory. The Earth-Dog could take their sense of honor!

The other dogs were barking their opinions at both of them, making suggestions that were almost entirely useless. "Not a fair move," Lucky heard in Fiery's deep bark. "Don't let him get hold of you like that, Snap."

"Keep her on the run, Lucky," Twitch yelped, and Lucky twitched his ear in irritation—what did the other dog *think* he was trying to do?

Some dogs were simply yelping their support for Lucky or Snap—and mostly Snap, Lucky noticed. He let his eyes sail briefly over the watching dogs. The only one not barking or yelping encouragement was Omega.

The little dog just sat on his haunches, watching everything through narrowed eyes—somehow as if he wasn't seeing the fight at all.

Lucky turned back to his opponent, feeling himself beginning to tire. He had to finish this.

As Snap bared her teeth once more, he was ready; he didn't want those sharp white fangs in his hide again, but he had to tempt her in. This time, when she leaped for him, he didn't sidestep her but let her fasten on his shoulder, then whipped his head around to grab the same ear he'd wounded before. Snap howled, but Lucky gave her no time to plead with Sweet. He flung her onto her back and pinned her down with a forepaw to her throat. Her legs kicked and scrabbled, but her claws couldn't reach his belly.

Through a mouthful of ear he snarled, "Yield!"

Snap yelped with pain and fury, but he released her ear only to snatch a fold of skin at her throat. He shook her. "Yield!"

Very suddenly, Snap went limp, and her tail thudded on the ground behind him. She lifted her paws, letting them hang in the air as she sullenly growled, "I yield."

The clearing was absolutely silent, every pair of eyes fixed on them as Lucky released Snap and stepped back. The tan-and-white dog rolled onto her paws and struggled up, shaking off the indignity. Her flanks heaved, but so did his. They were both panting from the struggle.

A great gray shadow paced between the ranks of watching

dogs; it was the first time Lucky had seen Alpha get off his rock for anything other than to eat or sleep, or to fight. Lucky gave him a wary glance, but the dog-wolf sat down on his haunches beside Sweet, looking from one combatant to the other.

"Impressive," he rumbled, his yellow eye sparking with fire, "for a City Dog. Snap, you are now demoted one rank. Lucky takes your place as hunter."

Lucky risked eye contact with his defeated opponent. She was expressionless, and for a horrible moment he thought she might fly at him again, or attack when he turned his back. But after one long, cool look, she lowered her ears and dipped her head.

"I will ask him to teach me some of those City Dog moves, Alpha," she remarked dryly. "Congratulations, Lucky."

A flood of relief went through him, together with a thrill at his victory. Lucky let his tongue loll, baring his teeth happily, and lowered his head to accept her lick. "I will be glad to show you a few. If you teach me to move as fast as you can."

"Done." Snap's jaw opened cheerfully too.

"Yes, you both fought well. Now you can stop stroking each other's backs," snapped Alpha. "As for the rest of the Pack: It has been clear that Lucky was needed on the patrol, in place of Moon, but he's a hunter now. Mulch?"

Startled, the black dog took a pace forward. "Yes, Alpha?"

"You are now demoted," said the dog-wolf brusquely. "You will patrol with Dart and Twitch from this no-sun."

"What?" Mulch's surprise and anger must have got the better of his good sense. "Alpha, that is not fair! Demote *Spring*; she's lower than me!"

Lucky heard a faint rumble of anger from Twitch's sister, but she kept her head bowed and her eyes low. She knew better than to stick her snout into another dog's argument with Alpha.

"Not anymore," Alpha growled. "Beta, explain to Mulch that he should not question my decisions."

Sweet bounded forward to give Mulch's nose a sharp bite that drew blood. He sat back on his haunches, shocked, his eyes dazed with pain, and she gave him a clout with her paw for good measure.

"Moon's pup Fuzz could have understood that," she told him sharply. "So I hope you can. Understand?"

"Yes, Beta," he whined.

"You have not been my best hunter," said Alpha, with more than a hint of threat in his voice, "to put it mildly. If you are so keen to climb the ranks, you should try harder, instead of whining about other dogs."

Lucky had got his breath back after the fight, but the tension in the camp was making his flanks heave nervously. *I just wanted to rise a few ranks,* he thought. *I didn't mean to cause all of this.*

"I'll see how he does on patrol," Sweet barked. "And take that look off your face, Mulch. You have had this coming since you tried to take Snap's place in the feeding. Accept it and learn—it will make you a better dog in the future."

Mulch was trembling as Alpha and Sweet stalked back to the central rock, but Lucky knew it wasn't only from fear. Sure enough, as soon as they were out of earshot, Mulch slunk to his side.

"You did this to me," he snarled in Lucky's ear. "Watch your scabby back, City Dog."

Lucky watched him creep away, all the more glad that it was not Mulch who he had challenged. *That could have gotten even nastier. . . .*

He did not have time to dwell on Mulch's animosity, because the rest of the Pack was crowding around him—even Snap— wagging their tails and giving him friendly barks and licks, congratulating him on his rise in status.

"You really deserve it," said Twitch. "That was some impressive fighting." Lucky saw Moon and Fiery exchange a skeptical glance—did they think he had used unfair moves?—but soon Dart and Spring had blocked them from his view as they eagerly added their praises.

Even as he yelped and licked them in return, Lucky could not shake the feeling that the dogs were seeking his favor to ensure that he did not pick on them in the future.

They're watching their own backs, Lucky thought. *Every wag of their tails is . . . tactical.* Unlike the Leashed Dogs, Alpha's followers were not bound together by affection, but by dependence. Personal loyalty was not as important as survival.

Lucky bit back a whine of frustration and confusion. *I'm not sure I like the struggle against one another here,* he thought. *But does this Pack have a better chance of surviving?*

CHAPTER FIFTEEN

"*Where do you think you're going,* Lucky?" Spring turned to blink at him, one ear cocked and one paw raised. "You're not sleeping in that drafty old patrol den anymore."

Once again he felt the stares of the whole Pack on him, and Lucky's skin went hot beneath his fur. Retreating from his old sleeping place, he followed Spring and Snap to a larger pile of leaves in the cozier shade of the hunting dogs' den. The snug hollow had been scraped deeper and filled with moss and rotted bark as well as leaves and soft pine branches, and it was certainly a good few paw-paces up from the beds of the patrol dogs.

As he turned his ritual circle, Lucky sent a prayer to the Forest-Dog for safety in his sneaky deception. The Sun-Dog and the Moon-Dog might not approve of what he had just done to Mulch—maybe even the Sky-Dogs would not like it—but he hoped the Forest-Dog at least would appreciate the daring that had lifted him in the ranks, the cunning and trickery that was preserving his fur so far. In the Great Howl that night, Lucky had thought he caught the quick movement of the Forest-Dog running through the undergrowth and felt for a moment a sense of approval, warm as the sun.

The recess where he settled to sleep reeked of Mulch's dark and musky scent, and he felt a flash of guilt. But he couldn't allow that to last. Lucky was not happy that he had to deceive them, but he *had* played by the Pack rules—and that was what Mulch must do too. If he wanted his place back, thought Lucky sternly, he could fight for it.

Fiery's bulk shifted beside him as the huge dog grunted and began snoring. He had been no more friendly to Lucky after the fight, but at least he had not been antagonistic either. Snap and Spring, who slept on his other side, had welcomed him into the hunting division with some warmth.

"We can use your quick moves hunting," Snap had said, as Spring wagged her agreement. "And your cleverness as well." Lucky admired Snap enormously for that. The rest of the Pack—the patrol dogs and the humble little Omega—had definitely gained respect for him, and they had treated him with deference today, though he was glad to realize his friendship with Twitch still seemed intact.

There was only one problem, he realized with a horrible suddenness. He wasn't on patrol anymore . . . so sneaking out of the camp to see Bella was going to be more difficult from now on. Lucky felt a burning tingle in his belly—he had got so caught up in rising through the ranks, he hadn't stopped to consider that he might actually be creating a problem for himself. Resting his muzzle on his forepaws, he pricked his ears and gazed up at the stars. How many nights had it been since he'd seen Bella? The Leashed Dog Pack could be in serious trouble, and he would have no idea.

They could also have found clean water of their own by now. What if Bella came out every night to meet Lucky, to tell him that it was fine to return, that he did not have to spy on the Wild Pack anymore, but Lucky could not get the message because he could not speak with his litter-sister? Would he be stuck here, in Alpha's Pack, forever?

And would that *really* be a bad thing?

He heaved a sigh. The black sky of no-sun was clear and cloudless, the stars pinpricks of glittering clear-stone. Lucky could make out all the constellations: the wily Rabbit, the Wolf and her Cub, the Great Tree, and the Running Squirrel. They seemed to spin above him, whirling and taunting, until his eyelids began to droop and sleep fuzzed his brain.

Distantly, a sound pierced his doze: the caw of a crow among the trees. In an instant Lucky was awake again. On one side of him Fiery snored mightily; on the other, heaped against each other, Snap's and Spring's flanks rose and fell with the steady rhythm of deep sleep.

He'd never known crows to be so fond of no-sun. But it reminded him he wanted to try to see Bella, to find out if he needed to go on with this deception. The Moon-Dog was climbing the sky now.

Heart pounding, Lucky eased up and slunk between the others' sleeping forms. His breath caught in his throat when Fiery's leg twitched twice, but after a moment the big dog's snores rumbled again like the Sky-Dogs' thunder. He was just dreaming.

Stepping carefully on the softest moss and moldy leaves, Lucky picked his way with painful slowness out of the hunters' den. From the position of the Great Tree and the height of the Moon-Dog, he thought it must be Dart's turn on watch; but she was looking for enemies trying to get into the camp. She would never expect an enemy trying to sneak *out*.

All he had to do was stay low, keep to the undergrowth, and be silent. So long as he did not trip over Dart as she made her rounds, he should be able to get safely away from the clearing. Then it was an easy run to the longpaw camp, and he would have plenty of time before the Moon-Dog yawned and went to sleep.

A twig cracked under his paw, and his heart almost stopped. But no dog stirred, and he placed one paw after another cautiously, scared with every step that he would make a noise that would wake one of his Pack. He had to crouch low to avoid the branches, too, and that did not make it any easier to be silent. But at last he was beyond the thickest of the undergrowth, and could stand tall again, and spring into a scamper.

It was a relief to stretch his legs and run, after the dreadful, tense creep-and-crawl out of the camp. Lucky breathed in the cool air of no-sun as he bounded through the trees and across the meadow. The stars above him, the solid ground beneath his feet, and the smell of the forest: This was perfect. This was how he was meant to be. Free and happy. No one watching him or expecting his aid. Alone!

Craaarrrk!

That no-sun crow again! Now he remembered seeing it before on his travels, and he was more certain than ever that it was a messenger of the Forest-Dog, sent to keep him in order.

He wished he could understand its messages better.

His happy heart plummeted when he caught the first scent of

the longpaw camp, and he slowed to a jogging pace, then a steady plod. *Oh, Sky-Dogs, what am I doing?*

Once inside the camp he stood still beside an overturned table, sniffing the air. It was hard to tell through the old reek of charred wood and meat, but he was sure Bella was not here. A wasted journey, then.

So why did he feel this swamping sense of relief?

Lucky was tempted to pad away as fast as he could. If Bella had not made it here tonight, that was not his fault. He could put off his treachery for another journey of the Sun-Dog.

He had already begun to turn when a flash of pale fur caught his eye. Hesitating, he looked back. Two small, familiar figures were squirming out from beneath another toppled table, panting with excitement.

"Lucky!" Sunshine's yelp was quieter than usual, he was glad to hear.

"Sunshine. Daisy!" Despite his uneasiness, Lucky felt his heart stir with warmth at the sight of the two Leashed Dogs. He crouched to lick their faces as they both jumped up to greet him. Then his heartbeat skipped. "Where is Bella? Has something happened to her?"

"No, no—nothing bad has happened!" Sunshine whined

happily as she nuzzled his nose. "Bella's fine. She sent us to meet you."

Daisy jumped in. "She has a special mission of her own. So she sent us in her place!" Lucky could see that the little dog was almost bursting with pride.

Lucky felt his eyes narrow. "What is she up to now?" It was not like Bella to hand over control to the most junior members of her Pack; he was sure she would have wanted to talk to him himself if she could.

"Bella has a brilliant plan," said Daisy. "We have to trust her!"

Lucky cocked his head doubtfully—*Bella's recent "brilliant plans" have brought us a lot of trouble*—but the little dogs' eyes gleamed with suppressed excitement. He could not cope with any more scheming, anyway; not right now, when he was still deep in the heart of the Wild Pack. Whatever it was, Bella could deal with it on her own this time.

"All right. I will tell you what I have seen." He licked his chops. "Will you remember it all to take back to Bella?"

"Between us we will," yelped Daisy eagerly.

It seemed he had little choice. It felt strange reporting back to these two inexperienced Leashed Dogs, especially now that he had lived with a true disciplined Pack, but he carefully recounted all that he had done and seen since he last spoke to Bella, including the terrifying encounter with the yellow-furred longpaws, his challenge to Snap, and his promotion.

"But that . . . that is so strange," said Sunshine, awed. "Do you have to fight all the time in that Pack?"

Lucky squirmed inwardly. "Not all the time, Sunshine. Just . . . when we want to rise in the Pack." Said like that, to these friendly dogs with their easygoing solidarity, it sounded silly and aggressive.

But Daisy cheered him. "Oh, Lucky! You're so brave!" She gave a happy yelp. "And so clever!"

Sunshine panted up at him, adoring, her misgivings instantly forgotten. "Now you will be able to find out even more about our enemies!"

"Yes . . ." Lucky found he didn't like that phrase. The Wild Pack did not *feel* like his enemies—most of them, anyway. And he did not want enemies any more than he wanted a Pack.

The two went together, he supposed.

"We will let Bella know," yapped Daisy. "She will be so proud of you!"

Lucky ignored this, and asked, "How is Bruno? And Martha?"

Sunshine's dark eyes veered away, as if the edge of the clearing was suddenly the most interesting thing in the world. Daisy sat back and scratched her belly.

"They are getting better, but they need more time. Martha's leg wound was really very, very bad."

"And Bruno was so unwell," put in Sunshine. "Thank the Sky-Dogs that you were there to save him, Lucky, or he might have choked!"

Lucky whined in confusion. "They should be getting better by now. Especially Martha . . ."

"Oh, there was some poison in her leg. Maybe from swimming! She is getting better, but it's taking longer than we thought it would."

Sunshine still avoided meeting his eye, and Lucky felt a tremor of sick anxiety in his belly. Poison in a wound? That might get better if Martha licked it well, but what if the poison got too deeply into her leg? And Bruno . . .

"They are going to be fine, Lucky. Don't worry."

Sunshine, usually so full of drama whether it was good or bad, sounded quite flat. Lucky could not shake the feeling that she was lying to him—but why? Could the news be worse than they were letting on? It seemed the only explanation: that they were trying to protect him from some kind of horrible truth.

Martha, Bruno. You came so far with me. Please be all right.

Did he have time to go back to Bella's Pack and see for himself? The Moon-Dog was padding languidly across the sky, the time of no-sun coming to an end. But perhaps . . .

"Lead me to the camp," he told them. "I really should talk to Bella. And maybe I can help Martha and Bruno."

"She's not finished with her mission," Daisy yipped, her tongue lolling. "And the Sun-Dog will be up and running soon."

Lucky whined his agreement. He did have to get back to the hunters' den.

I'll just have to trust Sunshine and Daisy.

"Then I guess I should get back," he said, "before anyone wakes up and realizes I'm gone." He licked Daisy's ears affectionately. "When I do come back, I'll have some great hunting tricks to show everybody. We will never be hungry again."

"You'll be a terrific teacher, Lucky," Daisy said. "You always are."

"It has been so good to see you, Lucky!" yipped Sunshine. She looked mournful. "We miss you a lot. Especially me and Daisy."

"That's why we offered to come in Bella's place," said Daisy with a whine of agreement.

"I miss you, too," Lucky assured them, caressing their heads fondly with his tongue. "But it will not be forever. I'll be back as soon as I can." *I hope so, anyway.*

As he licked and yipped his farewells and trotted away into the woods again, he felt sick with worry.

Earth-Dog, we already lost Alfie. Surely you can't want two more of my friends. Not now.

Lucky could barely focus on the sounds of the forest around him, on the stir of leaves and the rustle of small beasts in the undergrowth. It was only when a bigger shadow flickered through the bushes that he was finally jolted out of his unhappy thoughts.

Another longpaw? he thought, his heart thudding.

No, too small for a longpaw. All the same, Lucky stopped, ears pricked, and gave a soft growl.

A small fox, perhaps, on its nightly hunt. As long as it was alone, and had not brought friends, it was not a threat Lucky needed to worry about. . . .

But the shadow was creeping closer through the dense bracken, and from its rustling and occasional snuffling he could tell it was not nearly as cautious as a fox. Stiffening, Lucky yipped a challenge.

A squat, ugly little face shoved out through the leaves. It was not a fox, but the black eyes glinted with just as much cunning.

"Omega," breathed Lucky, shocked. "What are you doing out here?"

"I could ask *you* the same question," said Omega, his bark high-pitched and impudent. "You are not a patrol dog anymore. Are you, Lucky?"

"I . . . I . . ."

"You don't have to explain yourself to me," said Omega. "I *saw* you sneaking out of the camp."

Lucky thought his heart had actually stopped beating. Omega looked so smug, and the instinctive knowledge struck Lucky that if any member of the Pack had to find him out, Omega was the worst. "I just needed to be alone for a bit."

"Is that right?" That glint in Omega's eye was not friendly. "If you needed to be alone, why were you meeting up with the Leashed Dogs?"

Lucky instinctively glanced over his shoulder before he realized that he had just confirmed Omega's suspicions. His heart thudded in his chest as his panic rose. "But I didn't—"

"Yes, you did, you Liar Dog. Did you enjoy spending time with the little fluffy dogs? All that licking! Ugh!"

He did see me.

Omega sounded unbearably smug. "You are a spy for that

Pack. I have known all about it right from the start."

No! thought Lucky. *That is not possible!*

There was a horrible trickle of suspicion in his gut, though. That scent he had caught, when he and Bella had first discussed her plan . . . the half-drowned smell he could not quite place, the paw prints he could not identify. Could it have been Omega, sneaking around alone, ignored by his Pack as always?

"You spied on us!" Lucky exclaimed, and instantly knew how stupid that sounded.

"I do not spy," Omega sneered. "*I'm* better than that."

Lucky had nothing to say. There was nothing he *could* say. He did not know which was stronger: the fear, or the horrible shame.

"I was confused in the storm," the small dog went on. "The rain was so fierce that night, I thought the River-Dog was going to rise and drown the whole world. I got lost and I wanted to hide until it was over. It was your bad luck I happened to be hiding near you and your friend."

"Bad luck," echoed Lucky bleakly.

"Bad luck. Well, either that or the Sky-Dogs led me to you."

I would not be surprised, Lucky thought. *They probably never approved of what I was doing. . . .* "You're going to tell the others, I suppose?"

He wondered how fast he could get himself and Bella's Pack

away from here, and how far they would have to go to be safely beyond the fury of Alpha.

"Actually, I haven't decided yet." Omega sat down and scratched an ear in satisfaction. "A lot depends on you."

Lucky did not think his heart could sink further, but he was wrong. It plummeted like a heavy stone in still water. "What do you mean?"

"If you help me, I'll help you." Omega snickered. "Well, at least I won't get you killed. I do not like being Omega. I'm not Omega; my name is Whine."

Lucky swallowed. His spit tasted of fear, but he understood the small dog's attitude. He would not want to lose his own name, be called "Omega" in that contemptuous way by the whole Pack. It had never even occurred to him to ask the Omega what his real name was, and he felt ashamed of it now. "I wouldn't like it, either," he admitted.

"I want a proper place in the Pack." Omega padded back and forth, licking his chops. His face was so squashed and ugly, drool kept escaping and dripping from his jaws. "I have been Omega for far too long—taking orders, fetching, and carrying! And half-starving too, since nobody ever leaves enough food for me!"

"I tried to—"

"Not very hard. Not when Sweet ordered you to stop. And why would you leave food for an Omega anyway? Every Pack needs an Omega. I just want it to be a dog who is not me."

Lucky remembered the way the other Pack members treated the flat-nosed dog: as if he were barely a dog at all, sometimes. They would have given more respect to a sharpclaw.

"I want to help, but what can I do?" he said, cocking his head sympathetically. And he really did want to help. It was not just that he felt sorry for Omega; the simple fact was, he could not let this ugly, sneaky dog go back and tell Alpha his secret. He had to make some kind of a deal—it was that, or kill the little dog.

And Lucky knew there was no way he could ever do that.

And that is one more reason why I will never be fit for Pack life. I certainly could never be an Alpha. The thought did not displease him. It probably went against his dog-spirit—and no doubt it was a result of his Lone Dog life and his bond with the Leashed Dogs—but at least he knew that he would never sink so low as to kill another dog.

Lucky sighed. "It is a pity you're not with the Leashed Pack yourself," he remarked. "You would be happier there. No dog has to be Omega in their camp."

"I am no Leashed Dog." Omega's squat muzzle wrinkled even more with contempt. "But I will be of higher status than I am now, and you are going to help me get my promotion."

"I want to help you, Whine. And I suppose I don't have a choice, anyway."

"No," Whine grumbled arrogantly.

"I still don't see what you think I can do for you."

"It should be obvious—especially to a Street Dog like you." Whine licked idly at a paw. "Nothing I do is ever going to impress Alpha. I can't lie to myself about that. But if another dog behaves badly enough, or does something really stupid or dangerous . . ."

"Alpha will demote *that* dog to Omega," Lucky finished, a chill running through his fur.

"Exactly. Oh, and you shouldn't panic—I am not expecting *you* to sacrifice yourself. If I asked that, you might just kill me."

I would not, thought Lucky, *but I'm glad you have that wrong.*

"Since you are a hunter now, you will be perfectly placed. When you bring back food tomorrow, all you have to do is make it look as if another dog has stolen some before the others get to it. You know how much Alpha hates that."

"Yes . . ." agreed Lucky dismally.

"Anyone who eats before Alpha is going to go straight to the bottom of the heap."

Anyone who eats before Alpha will be fortunate if that is all that happens to them, thought Lucky. "Why can't you just do it yourself?"

"Because I have *you* to do it for me, obviously. Look, the risk is much less for you; you must see that. If you get caught in the act, you will be demoted, but you'll soon have clean paws again. You can do something clever, or keep using your charm on Beta. Dogs like you are always . . ." He gave an amused whine as he finished his sentence: " . . . *lucky.*" Sitting down, thumping his stubby tail, Whine wrinkled the corner of his mouth.

"Do not insult me," snarled Lucky, ignoring the sting of truth. "Remember, for this to work, you need me!"

"You need me even more. Or rather, you need me to be *nice* to you." Whine's eyes gleamed with arrogant triumph. "You know I'm right, Street Dog. You wouldn't be risking nearly as much as I would."

Lucky took a deep breath. He knew he could not lose his temper.

"If it happens, you will work your way back up eventually," Whine went on. "But how can Alpha demote a dog who is already at the bottom? It would be simpler for him to just kill me."

Lucky knew in the pit of his stomach that Whine was right. He had no choice. There was no way he could allow the Omega dog to reveal his secret, or it was Lucky who would probably be killed. So yet again, he was going to have to do the bidding of another dog, and if anything this job was even more dishonorable than the one that Bella had given him. Lucky felt a surge of desire to be on his own again, free of all these terrible demands that were being placed on him.

Why did I get myself into this?

In fact, he did feel sorry for Whine, despite his cunning and his dangerous threats. Maybe it was time someone else took a turn at being Omega—they would soon work their way back up the Pack once more, but at least Whine would have had a taste of higher status, and might even be encouraged to try harder in the future.

"All right," he said at last.

"I knew you would help!" For a moment Whine looked happy, his eyes bulging with excitement. His tail thumped the ground, but then he seemed to realize he was giving too much away. He stilled and closed his smiling jaws. "Thank you. I will see you back at the camp. And be quick."

With a new bounce in his step, Whine turned and trotted off into the undergrowth. Lucky sagged with relief as he watched him go, but he could not calm the churning misery inside him.

Who was he going to target? He had friends and comrades in the Pack; they trusted him.

But I have no choice!

He was more certain than ever that, as soon as he could free himself from both of these Packs, he was leaving. He was going back to being a Street Dog, a Lone Dog—a happy dog.

In the meantime, he had to go through with all his deceptions. *I am doing this for Bruno and Martha,* he told himself firmly. *It does not make me a bad dog, or an evil one. I'm just tangled up in a mess, and there are things I have to do to get out of it.*

It was all about survival for Lucky now.

The world has changed. For a skin-shivering instant, he thought the Forest-Dog himself had whispered in his ear.

Yes, the world *had* changed. And Lucky needed to do whatever it took to stay alive, to see the Sun-Dog rise and stretch again. Once he had achieved this, then . . .

Then he was going to be free of *all* of them.

CHAPTER SIXTEEN

Lucky watched as the patrols left camp the next day. He was resting in the snug hunters' den, Snap's warm back against his. Fiery was standing up and stretching in the misty morning light, his tail thumping slowly with contentment. Lucky pricked his ears, his nerves singing inside his skin as Mulch padded by. The black dog showed no open hostility, but there was a sullen look on his face as he glanced at Lucky.

Lucky found himself enjoying his new status, now that Twitch wasn't constantly dragging him out to check the boundaries or keep an alert eye on Moon and the pups. His first long, lazy day as a hunter would have been easy and trouble-free, had his neck fur not prickled every time Omega slunk into sight. Once or twice the cringing dog cast Lucky a look that was sly and knowing. *Stop it!* Lucky thought. *You don't want any of the other dogs to notice.* He wasn't sure Omega was clever enough to hide his newfound satisfaction.

The Sun-Dog was loping lazily down the sky and the shadows

were lengthening by the time Fiery barked gruffly, summoning the hunters. Lucky didn't resent this command. His new role and higher status excited him; besides, his blood thrilled at the thought of a hunt. *Let's get started!* He was first to Fiery's side, and when Snap and Spring joined them they all trotted out of the camp with ears and tails held high.

The sunlight was still warm, and the Sun-Dog cast golden shadows that dappled the landscape and sprinkled the lake like glittering clear-stone. It could not have been a better evening for him to begin, Lucky thought: With any luck their prey would be drowsy and off-guard after the heat of the day. He hoped he'd make a good first impression, and prove himself worthy of his promotion.

Lucky was relieved to discover that Fiery was a good leader. He didn't waste time or effort bossing the other dogs about how to track scents or stay hidden. He trusted them to get on with their jobs. It was so different from Bella's pack, where Lucky'd had to go through the motions of beetle-catching over and over again for Sunshine's benefit. . . .

Fiery was a good hunter, too, even if he wasn't the cleverest of dogs. Watching him and Snap and Spring as they prowled was like watching three paws of a single dog. Lucky realized with pride that he was the fourth paw.

"Stop here," commanded Fiery in a low voice as they approached the edge of the forest. Lucky, Snap, and Spring halted and waited in alert silence. Fiery lifted his muzzle and sniffed the air, one paw raised and trembling slightly with anticipation. Snap and Spring watched him, patient and trusting, and Lucky was happy to go along with their instincts. Later, perhaps, he'd get a chance to prove his own individual skills—the way he could silently pad up to a prey, or snap a neck with his jaws.

At last Fiery glanced back at them all and nodded. "Twitch reported a few deer here this morning. Let's be quiet."

Lucky and Spring followed Fiery as Snap slunk quietly off to the side, soon disappearing into the undergrowth. Twitch had been right, Lucky realized as his nose prickled with the musky scent of large prey animals. He was determined not to let down the hunting group, but he was confident too. *I'm good at hunting, no matter how much they sneer at my old city life*. Deer were fast, sure enough—but so were rabbits, and a deer made a bigger target.

Spring melted away into the bushes to his left, so that Fiery and Lucky were the only dogs following the main trail. The pungent scent of deer was strong now. When Fiery nodded at him, Lucky knew immediately what to do; it wasn't unlike the times when he'd join up with other City Dogs, just for a hungry night or two, to hunt in a group. Lucky followed the rules and tricks he'd learned then; he separated from his leader, taking a wide circle but keeping Fiery in view.

A ray of sunlight through the branches burnished a furry golden flank; leaf and branch litter rustled beneath delicate hooves. Three of them, Lucky counted, and the deer were still browsing, unaware. He went entirely still as a slender head lifted to snuff the air. Suddenly there was alarm in the buck's huge, dark eye.

But it wasn't Lucky's scent the buck had caught. It leaped with a flash of white tail, and the hinds followed, but they were fleeing from Spring at the far side of the clearing—and toward Lucky. The buck bounded, crashing through bracken and brush, the two hinds following in a panic, but one hind was slower than the other, and was dashing in a straight line between Fiery and Lucky.

Lucky's blood raced as he smelled her fear, his muscles tightening. He sprang at the same time as Fiery, and they fell on the hind together. Lucky's teeth closed on her flank as Fiery seized her throat, and the deer stumbled and went down with a high squeal of terror.

Lucky held on grimly on as she kicked and struggled, but Snap and Spring were with them now too, piling onto the struggling prey. As Fiery held the hind down, her eyes lost their terrified light and she sank down into the undergrowth, kicking feebly. Lucky couldn't help feeling a thrill of pleasure at their success. They'd hunted well.

When the fight had gone from the hind completely, and she went limp and heavy with death, Fiery drew back. He was panting with effort, but clearly pleased.

"Well done, Lucky," he said gruffly. "And you two. That was fine flushing."

"Alpha's going to be happy with this," Snap barked.

"Don't relax," growled Fiery. "He will be happy, but we can do better. Let's prove it! The gopher meadow next. Spring, you guard this prey."

Fiery was right. As Lucky had suspected, it was a particularly good evening for hunting: warm enough to draw out small animals into the open, but with a light breeze that kept the dogs' scent from their prey. They caught two rabbits and a sleepy gopher before Fiery was content, and even as they returned to Spring and the deer, Snap caught sight of a weasel that froze and bared its teeth before losing its nerve. When it scurried into a rabbit burrow Lucky thought they'd lost their prey, but Snap wormed her way after it and reemerged with an earth-spattered head and a limp stoat in her jaws.

She's surprisingly nimble, thought Lucky in admiration. *I don't know many dogs who could have followed a weasel down that hole. Or many dogs who would have dared. . . .*

Spring, still dutifully guarding the dead deer, barked a greeting as they trotted back to her with their haul. "No trouble. A fox liked the look of this deer, but I made him change his mind!"

"Good," said Fiery. "I knew I could count on you, Spring. Now let's get back to the Pack. The pups are growing fast now, and Moon will be hungry."

There was a note of fierce pride in the huge dog's voice, and Lucky felt a new affection for Fiery—and his pups—steal into his heart. Besides, he'd seen how Spring's rib cage swelled with pleasure at Fiery's compliment. The big brown dog was a fine leader in all kinds of ways.

Alpha and Sweet and Fiery each have their own methods, he mused. *Their ways are different. But all of them manage their parts of the Pack unchallenged.* Lucky stored the knowledge away. *I'm not going to be in a Pack forever, but still—there are lessons here worth learning.*

It was hard work dragging the deer back to camp together

with the rest of their prey, but Fiery was big enough to do most of the heavy work, helped by Lucky. He took hold of a hoof in his jaws and pulled it along, the hardness of the hoof clattering against his teeth. The other dogs gripped the smaller prey. Saliva pooled in Lucky's mouth at the taste of deer flank, but he knew better than to risk a bite—and he was surprised to find himself unwilling to take any share before he was with his Pack. *Strange,* he thought, *but it does feel right to wait. . . .*

The feeling intensified inside him when they reached the camp, where the other dogs bounded out to greet them with delight. They barked and whined in excitement, praising the hunters' skills and yelping with appreciation.

"Well done!" Twitch said, looking at Lucky.

"That will feed all of us—with leftovers!" Dart agreed.

"Moon will be pleased," Fiery said smugly, letting the deer fall. "Our pups are getting big and hungry."

Lucky's proudest moment, though, was when Sweet padded up to him and licked his ear. "Fiery told me how much you contributed to this catch," she murmured. "I'm glad you rose to be a hunter, Lucky."

They dumped their prey beside a pine at the edge of the camp and Lucky withdrew and lay down, panting. He was tired, but it was a good sort of exhaustion from a job well done. His feelings were mixed as he watched the rest of the Pack play and squabble and stretch aching limbs. He was still so worried about Martha and Bruno, not to mention his uncertainty about Bella's intentions, but he couldn't help this sense of contentment that stole over him. It was good to have a role here, to know his place, and to be appreciated for the skills he brought with him.

He thought back to Bella's Pack and the chaos that sometimes took over, the way the other dogs had all expected him to lead them in the early days. *Sometimes I just want to be given a job to do,* he thought. *Be part of a team. Not the dog making the decisions.* Of course, Bella was that dog now—but even so. There was part of him that still felt the heavy responsibilities of being involved in that Pack. Here, he didn't have to take charge of anything, and there was something in him that liked it that way.

The bushes rustled, and abruptly his peace was broken. Lucky didn't even have to turn to know who was sidling up to him. His hackles rose automatically, and he stiffened but lay still.

"Hello, Whine," he murmured. "What do you want?"

The little Omega snuffled and licked his chops. "Why, Lucky. I just wanted to ask if there was anything our fine hunter needs?"

"Nothing. Thank you."

"I can bring you anything, as you know. That's my job."

Lucky turned his head sharply. He mustn't anger the snub-faced dog—and that very fact made Lucky angry with himself.

"No, Whine, thank you."

"You must call me Omega," the dog said, with a submissive little whimper that sounded mocking to Lucky's ears. "For now. Until you do what you promised to do, City Dog."

Lucky turned his head, tempted to nip him whatever the consequences, but Omega had vanished into the tree shadows once more. Unhappiness roiled in Lucky's belly; his earlier haze of contentment had vanished altogether.

Omega wasn't going to forget the promise he'd forced Lucky to make, and Lucky couldn't risk Omega telling what he knew. He'd have to eat some of this prey—steal the food he'd been so proud to bring to the Pack—and make one of the other dogs suffer for his own crime.

It has to be the deer, he realized, with a hollow sense of shame. The deer was the most impressive thing the hunters had brought back in days. With that on display, its smell and size so tempting, Alpha might not even notice something like a missing gopher leg. *My crime has to be so bad that the other dogs are stunned.*

He dreaded the horrible task. *You are a liar, Lucky. A liar and a spy and a cheat.*

But he had no choice.

Who to frame, though? Whose life should I destroy? Lucky glanced around the Pack, keeping his face calm and disinterested despite the turmoil in his innards. *Who am I going to sacrifice, just to keep myself and my lies safe and hidden?*

One thing was so clear in his head it hurt: When the choice was made, he'd have to go ahead immediately. No more delays; no more excuses.

Maybe that was why he was putting off the moment of decision. But it didn't matter how often his eyes roamed the other dogs: The choice had been obvious from the start.

Mulch.

Mulch was a known food-stealer. Mulch had pawed selfishly at that rabbit, had tried to sneak an extra portion out of turn. No one would be very surprised if it was Mulch who stole a mouthful or two of deer before it was time to eat. And horribly, Lucky was already plotting the details of his deception. Mulch had long, shiny black hair, distinctive among the others of the Pack. There were already strands of it all over his new sleeping-place among the patrol dogs, but even better—or worse—there were still plenty of them in the hunter's den. The very bed Lucky now slept in was lined with Mulch's molted hairs. How hard could it be to transfer some of those long rippling strands to the deer's pale-gold hide?

How hard can it be, Lucky?

Lucky closed his eyes and shoved his nose beneath his paws, feeling sick. He tried to remember how unfriendly Mulch had been to him since he arrived, but it was no good: He still couldn't bear to think of what he was about to do to an innocent dog.

Strangely enough, what he was about to do to the Pack seemed even worse. He was going to betray their trust, to sow resentment and hatred, to lie to his Packmates. He was more like them than he'd ever known before he began this game of Bella's. He respected them, liked them, trusted them with his life each day . . .

I can't do it. I CAN'T.

But I must, a small, cowardly voice inside him whispered. *I have to do this, or I'll die.*

A great sigh escaped from the depths of his belly. He wasn't just doing this for his own survival—he was doing it to help the Leashed Dogs. He opened his eyes again to gaze around at the Pack.

They're not like me; they're NOT. I don't care. I'm a Lone Dog and I always will be. I survive. That's what I do.

It comes down to one thing. Do I want to go back to being who I really am? Or do I want to give all that up, to be a Pack Dog, to be like Fiery, or Snap, or Sweet . . .

Or Omega.

Lucky shivered. No, he couldn't be lulled into Pack life, just for the fun of a group hunt on a warm evening, or the bone-deep thrill of a Great Howl. Omega could not be allowed to tell his secret; he had to survive, to escape, to be Lucky again. Whatever he had to do must be done. That was all.

I'm never going to feel good about this, he thought, *but I'll just have to live with it—if I want to live at all. Because I'm Lucky, Lone Dog Lucky, and I'm going to survive.*

Before he could gnaw it over for another instant, Lucky stood up. He took a deep breath. Then, shaking himself, stretching lazily and clawing the ground, he padded idly over to the hunters' den and began to scrape at his own soft hollow, as if simply adjusting it to his needs.

Surreptitiously he nosed a few tangled bits of Mulch's hair into a straggly pile. With a deep breath, he licked it into his jaws. It caught on the sensitive flesh inside his mouth, tickled his throat. Lucky wanted to gag, but the horrible sensation of the hair against his teeth was as much to do with his feelings, he decided, as the taste of Mulch's fur.

It didn't matter how carefully he checked that no one was watching; as he crept through scrub toward the tree where the food lay, he felt as if every eye in the Pack was on him—two yellow ones in particular. *Don't look around. Behave naturally!* But when he cast a last glance over his shoulder, he was as sure as he could be that he hadn't been seen. Alpha lay on his favorite rock, his eyes closed and Sweet curled against him. The others were relaxing, grooming one another, exchanging the day's news, settling arguments, playing idle games, or staging mock-fights. The larger of the male pups, Squirm, was wrestling with his sister, Nose, nipping at her with his harmless milk teeth, while the smaller male, Fuzz, chased his tail determinedly, his short legs scrabbling in the dirt. Moon and Fiery watched them proudly, their attention fully focused on their pups.

It was now or never, and never was not an option. Lucky brushed his tongue against the deer's flank, trying to dislodge the hairs in his mouth. He spat and dribbled as best he could, but though some of the hairs had stuck to the deer, more of them had stuck to his teeth, caught in the gaps between them.

No! Lucky began to panic, pawing at his muzzle, clawing at his teeth, all the time trying not to look too agitated in case one of the other dogs noticed. The hairs were sticky and stubborn, clinging to his tongue and the soft skin inside his mouth till he wanted to be sick. And wouldn't that give him away, he thought, half in fear and half in a sort of excitable panic.

At last! One of his claws hooked into the tangled hair and pulled it free of his mouth, and he licked the rest of it against the deer's leg. He rubbed a last strand from his nose.

And now?

Lucky peered around the tree again, his breath in his throat, but still no one was paying any attention to him—not even Omega. *Whine's so sure of himself and his plotting,* Lucky thought with resentment.

There was no more time for guilt. Lucky tore into the deer's belly, ripping open a gash in the hide and then savaging the still-warm meat, gulping down great mouthfuls as fast as he could. He'd helped catch the creature, after all; his scent on the prey would be nothing strange.

He tore, gulped, swallowed; then did it again, and again. *Enough! Surely that's enough? One more bite. Quick, Lucky. HURRY.*

When he could bear the tension no longer, he sprang back

from the hind, his heart beating ferociously. Turning abruptly, he crept hurriedly through the trees and trotted away from the camp boundary.

I'm surprised I'm not falling over my own paws. He was furious at the way his skin and muscles trembled, and the anger helped drive out the fear, just a little.

He bounded to the lakeshore with his blood still racing. There was no time even to drink; he simply dipped his bloody muzzle into the cool water, washing away any possible last traces of Mulch's hair along with the deer blood. Then he loped silently around to the far side of the camp. He paused as long as he dared for breath, then wandered back in as coolly as he could.

If my Packmates could hear my heart, I'd be a dead dog in an instant. But it seemed none of them could. Slowly, so slowly, Lucky's heart stopped pounding, and he lay down in a new spot as if nothing had happened, as if he'd merely moved position out of restlessness.

I've gotten away with it.

Ecstatic relief was swamped almost immediately by horrible guilt, and the terror of what might have been. Noticing Omega slinking across the clearing, Lucky curled his muzzle and gave him a silent snarl that the little dog couldn't see.

He could not doze, as some of the other dogs were doing; his belly was full and his nerves and bones still throbbed with tension. They waited for Alpha's signal to eat, and Lucky felt dread growing with every instant. At last, when Lucky thought he could bear it no longer, Alpha blinked and yawned, rose and stretched, and Sweet stirred beside him.

The great dog-wolf leaped down from the rock and padded to the center of the clearing, his deep bark summoning his Pack.

"Now we eat."

It was the patrol dogs who dragged the prey into the open, and as soon as they did, Lucky saw them exchanging glances, their hackles rising and their tails stiffening. Far more nervously than usual, they dropped the food in the eating place, and hurried back from it as if they couldn't get away fast enough.

They've noticed. They've seen the damage!

They know trouble's coming. . . .

The hind's leg, stiff and straight, sank to the ground as the corpse settled, and Alpha stepped forward.

He stood stiff, foursquare, and silent, and the hush spread to the whole Pack.

The air of the clearing seemed to prickle with invisible fire as Alpha lowered his head to sniff the deer's flank. When he raised it again, his huge teeth were bared, and there was crackling fury in his eyes. Lifting his muzzle, he gave a howl of pure rage.

The silence that fell was unbroken by so much as a cracking twig. Even the birds were silent.

Alpha's growl was deadly.

"Who. Has. Done. This?"

CHAPTER SEVENTEEN

Alpha spun around, the look of violent fury on his face like nothing Lucky had ever seen.

"Who?"

The dog-wolf slammed a paw onto the ground. Jerking to one side, he spat something out. When he raised his head again, he was looking directly at Lucky.

The bolt of cold fear through his bones was so shocking, it was all Lucky could do not to cower and confess. He was desperate to scratch at his muzzle, to remove the black hair he was sure he must have left there. No . . . no, he couldn't have been so careless.

Could wolves read the minds of dogs? Did Alpha know?

Lucky wondered how fast he could run. Not fast enough . . .

The howl of confession was rising in his throat when Alpha took a pace forward. Not toward Lucky, though; his ice-cold eyes were locked on Mulch. With a great swipe of his paw, he sent a clod of earth flying into Mulch's muzzle. When the dirt settled, a hair lay balanced delicately on Mulch's nose.

The bewildered dog shook it off, making his long ears flap. "Alpha?"

Alpha didn't answer, but stalked menacingly close to him.

Mulch cowered. "Alpha, I don't know—"

"Silence!" The dog-wolf's muzzle curled. "Food-thief. Did you think it was your right to eat before Moon's pups? Before ME?"

Mulch's jaws hung open. "I didn't! I never—"

Alpha leaped for Mulch, bowling him over, clawing his face and neck, fangs sinking into his ears. Mulch gave a long howl of terror, scrabbling hopelessly to get out from under the huge beast. He was on his back now, and one of Alpha's hind legs raked cruel claws into his belly. Mulch's howl became a frantic series of agonized yelps.

Lucky wished he could put his paws over his ears. *Stop*, he wanted to bark. *It wasn't him, it was ME. . . .*

No, Lucky. SURVIVE.

The other dogs looked on, shivering, eyes wide, tails low and tight between their legs. Sweet was stiff and trembling at his side. Lucky glanced at her, hoping desperately that she would put a stop this. Drops of Mulch's blood spattered her face as she watched, and her muzzle wrinkled into a snarl.

Now, he thought frantically. *Stop him, Sweet, before it gets worse. No one else will....*

Suddenly the swift-dog leaped forward in a graceful spring, and Lucky almost gasped with relief. *She's stopping him! Oh, thank the Sky-Dogs—*

But he wasn't to get off so lightly, Lucky realized. He gaped as Sweet bared her teeth and sank them into the base of Mulch's tail, renewing his howls of pain. And then Sweet was attacking him too, her jaws snapping at those vulnerable ears as Alpha seized the folds of flesh at Mulch's neck and shook him like a rat.

Lucky couldn't stand it anymore. With a bark of protest he bounded toward the struggling Mulch, but when Sweet took her teeth from Mulch's ear to give him a warning glare, he came to a shocked halt. Her muzzle curled back from her bloodstained fangs, but that wasn't what brought him up short. He was sure he didn't imagine the softness in her dark eyes.

She doesn't want me to get hurt. She's protecting me!

Trembling, he stepped carefully back as Sweet renewed her assault, biting and scratching.

It felt like a turn of the Moon-Dog before Alpha finally clouted Mulch one last time on the head and stepped back, snarling softly. Sweet sat down beside Alpha, tongue lolling as she gazed at Mulch with contempt.

Mulch rolled onto his belly, but when he tried to crawl away he could only flop, his flanks heaving, a terrible high-pitched whimper coming from his throat. The rest of the Pack watched him with pity, but none of them, Lucky noticed, moved to help him.

"You," growled Alpha at the cringing, wounded dog, "are now Omega."

"Which is more than you deserve," added Sweet, licking blood idly from a forepaw.

"But, Alpha . . ." Mulch's breathless whine was barely audible.

"And since you feel inclined to argue, you may not challenge another dog until a full turn of the Moon-Dog." Alpha flicked the tip of his tail. "Your hairs were on the carcass, Omega. Your hairs. How dare you try to deny it?"

Mulch laid his head on his forepaws, doing his best to raise his haunches, miserably submissive. He had clearly decided it was not worth arguing anymore.

There was a slight coughing sound from the circle of watching dogs, and the former Omega crept forward a little. His bulging eyes flickered briefly to Lucky, but they held no expression.

Don't start thanking me, thought Lucky ferociously. *Don't you dare be so stupid!*

But the little dog was now gazing pathetically up at Alpha, who watched him in scornful silence for a few moments.

"Yes. I suppose you're a patrol dog now, Omega. Or Whine, as we will call you. For now." Turning his back, Alpha padded back toward the prey-heap.

Sweet cast a last disdainful glance at Whine before following her leader. "And try to prove yourself worthy, Whine. For the Sky-Dogs' sake, and your own."

Any appetite Lucky still had after the theft of the deer was gone. He couldn't take his eyes off Mulch as the beaten dog slunk into the bushes to lick his wounds. Lucky had to force himself to join the feeding, lying down miserably next to Twitch.

"Don't feel bad for Mulch," Twitch told him airily. "I mean, Omega. He deserved that."

He didn't, thought Lucky.

When Fiery and Spring had eaten their fill, Lucky had to creep forward and force himself to eat a second full meal, though he was afraid it might choke him. Doing his best to mask his disgust, he ripped mouthful after mouthful from his share of the carcass and gulped it down his tight throat. *I have to eat. It's supposed to be the first I've eaten all day. . . .*

If he had to bring it back up later, he'd do it in secret; but Lucky couldn't let the others suspect that he'd already eaten. There was a thin covering of leaf litter beneath the tree, and he managed to push a few bitefuls beneath that, but he couldn't risk Sweet seeing him do it, so most of it he had to choke down. His body heaved with the effort and he had to concentrate on each swallow. He couldn't even show his relief when he'd eaten enough, and could crawl back from what was left of the hind.

I don't think I'll ever enjoy deer again. . . .

After Snap, Twitch, and Dart had eaten, it was Whine's turn. Lucky had never seen a dog wolf down food with such relish, and he'd had no idea such a small, pathetic dog could cram so much meat into his belly. Obviously the pudgy creature's conscience was clear about what they had done. Despite the abundance of tonight's prey, despite what had been a huge bounty when the Pack began to eat, Whine left scarcely anything for Mulch, and Lucky felt his anger at the sly little dog grow darker and deeper.

If any dog ought to have had sympathy for the new Omega, it should have been the old one. Whine knew what it felt like to go hungry, to be despised and overlooked.

Surely he could have shown a little pity! Lucky felt his muzzle curl as he watched Whine's smug, flat face, still smeared with deer blood. *No, I can't think about him; I'll only get angrier, and I can't afford to do that.*

Lucky could only hope the Great Howl would make him feel better about himself, but as the dogs gathered and the eerie sound swelled into the night sky, his gaze was drawn against his will to Mulch. The newly appointed Omega was trying to join in, but his howls were faint and brief, and he was obviously too weak from his beating to take his Pack-place in the great bonding time. No shadow-dogs bounded across Lucky's vision that night; there was no enchantment in the Great Howl for him.

Mulch—Lucky found it impossible to think of him as Omega—was the first to slink away when the sounds of the Howl had died off. Lucky waited till the rest of the Pack had dispersed to their sleeping-places before he carefully retrieved the meat he'd hidden, then padded across to the uncomfortable shallow scrape where Mulch had to make his new bed. As the branches rustled, Mulch looked up at him, startled.

"What do you want?" There was resentment in the black dog's eyes.

"I brought—" Lucky took a breath. "I brought you food. There was some left."

"That's not allowed." Mulch glared at him suspiciously.

"No one's going to know." Lucky pawed the chunks of flesh closer to Mulch. "I'm certainly not going to confess to Alpha."

Just saying those words sent a tremor of guilt through his spine, but Mulch didn't notice. "Why would I take food from you?"

Lucky couldn't blame him. "You didn't get much."

"No. That little dung-scraping Whine didn't want to leave me any."

"It didn't seem fair. When there was so much today."

"No. It wasn't fair," grunted Mulch. His nose was stretching toward the food, however reluctant he seemed. "You're not trying to trick me, are you, City Dog?"

"Of course not," protested Lucky. *Not now, anyway.*

In the end Mulch couldn't help himself. He licked a few times at the meat, then dragged it closer and began to tear into it with his teeth. Lucky could barely watch. He'd eaten a good half of it before he glanced up again.

"Thank you," he growled, a little sadly. "Though I don't know why you'd help an Omega dog. Especially when I didn't exactly welcome you to the Pack."

And that's one of the reasons I picked you as my victim. Lucky swallowed. "I just . . . felt bad about it. I'm not used to Pack rules. Especially rules about Omegas."

"Well," said Mulch gruffly, "thank you anyway." He gulped

down more mouthfuls of flesh.

Leaving Mulch alone to eat the scraps of his own dinner, Lucky squeezed through the branches again and padded back to the hunters' den.

Forest-Dog, he thought unhappily, *please don't let Mulch get any smarter. Don't let him figure it out.*

Don't ever let him realize that all the trouble started when I arrived.

CHAPTER EIGHTEEN

It was too hot and close in the hunters' den, and after much squirming and circle-treading, Lucky gave up his attempts to sleep. He crept into the clearing to slump down on the cool grass. Above him, in the circle of the star-silhouetted pine tops, the Moon-Dog glowed fierce and full, spilling silver light that was bright enough to cast shadows. *Thank the Sky-Dogs that I'm not sneaking out to see Bella tonight,* thought Lucky. *I'd be seen straight away.*

Something moved at the other side of the clearing, catching his attention, and Lucky pricked his ears with curiosity. In the moonlight it was easy to see a huge shape emerge from the finest den of all, the one that was soft with long grass and sheltered by flat stone.

Alpha, thought Lucky in surprise, watching his leader pace restlessly across the clearing. The dog-wolf's eyes glowed as he gazed up at the Moon-Dog. Lucky's ears went forward in surprise as Alpha strode on and vanished between the trees.

Sweet's slender form appeared from the bushes and she stretched languidly before padding across to Lucky.

"Can't sleep?" She lay at his side, ears pricked, her eyes on the spot where Alpha had disappeared.

"No. I can't. Where has Alpha gone?"

She gave a low, perplexed growl. "He always leaves when the Moon-Dog reveals her full face—he wants to be alone with her for a time." Sweet shook her head as if she didn't really understand. "It's a habit he brought from his Wolf Pack days. They always sang to the Moon-Dog together, Alpha says. It was even more special than the Great Howl. Even more special," she repeated in disbelief.

Though he understood no more than Sweet did, Lucky felt a tingle in his backbone. He could barely imagine a sensation more thrilling than the Great Howl, but if that was true of the Moon-Dog ritual, it was no wonder Alpha wanted to recall a little of it, even though he had no Wolf Pack to share with. Once again Lucky wondered what could have driven Alpha to leave his wolf-comrades and run with a Pack of feral mutts.

Of course, one of those feral mutts had almost drawn Lucky into Pack life himself. . . .

Lucky gazed at Sweet's elegant head, raised to sniff the night air and perhaps to follow Alpha's scent trail too.

"Sweet," he said, "could you walk with me for a while?"

She turned her head and tilted an ear, studying him. "You mean, outside the camp?"

"Yes. I want to talk to you. Alone."

Sweet tapped her tail thoughtfully on the earth. "I'm not sure that's a good idea, Lucky. What would Alpha say if he knew?"

"From what you told me, he won't be back for a long time." Catching her doubtful expression, he pressed his advantage. "Do you have to do everything he says?"

Sweet tensed. "Certainly not. But he's my Alpha and I respect him."

"And he obviously respects you." *Cunning ploy, City Dog.* "And trusts you. I need to talk to you, that's all. And it's hard to do that when the Pack is all around."

Sighing, Sweet thought for a while, then gave a reluctant nod. "All right, Lucky. Just for a while, then." She stood up on her long legs. "The lakeshore, I think. It's a good place to talk."

Lucky padded at her flank as she slipped silently between the trees. They soon came to the long silver line of the lake's shore and heard the soft rush of its gentle waves on the pebbles. The Moon-Dog blazed a brilliant path across the water, making

225

the skyful of stars look dim in contrast.

They paused at the water's edge, letting waves tickle their forepaws. Suddenly tongue-tied, Lucky bent to lick at the wet fur between his claws, teasing out burrs with his teeth.

"What did you want to talk about?" asked Sweet, less impatiently than he expected. She cocked her ears, inclining her head to watch the rippling river of moonlight.

Lucky took a breath. "Was it really necessary? What you and Alpha did to Mulch?"

Sweet was silent for a moment; then she sighed and sat down on her haunches. "Yes. Yes, Lucky, it really was. In a Pack, things are sometimes necessary even when you don't like doing them."

"Didn't you?" He hesitated, not wanting to sound insolent, but wanting very much to know. "Like it, I mean?"

"Of course not." She was indignant now. "How could I enjoy something like that? It was my duty. I'm Alpha's partner and I have to stand by him. I have to support him in all things, especially where Pack discipline is concerned. If we weren't strong together, the Pack would fall apart."

The tide of bitter jealousy that raced through his blood receded, leaving a small seed of hope in his gut.

"Sweet. You said partner."

"Yes?"

"Partner. Not mate."

There was an expression in her dark eyes that he couldn't read at all. Lucky's fur prickled under her intense gaze.

"That's right," she said at last. "Partner."

"So it's strictly a Pack rank thing? It's your place in the hierarchy, not—"

"Exactly." She shook herself and turned back to her study of the lake.

"Sweet . . ." He paused, thumping his tail nervously. "I've wanted to ask you for a while. How did you rise so fast in the Pack?"

She sighed and splashed a paw in the shallow waves, scattering shards of light. "I don't really want to talk about it, Lucky. There was . . . well, there was another Beta before I arrived. We didn't . . . get along. She isn't around anymore."

The hair stood up on the back of Lucky's neck. To fill the awkward silence, he stood up on all four paws and lapped at the water. Presumably he could drink freely so long as he wasn't on patrol; it was deliciously cool against his tongue and throat.

"Alpha and I are a team." Sweet's voice broke the silence. "We work together, run the Pack, keep discipline, and keep it strong.

Maybe we'll become mates someday; that's what usually happens. But there's no hurry."

Lucky forced himself to keep drinking, and to focus on that one part: *There's no hurry.*

"I like my place in the Pack," she went on stubbornly. "I've never been a Beta before. I didn't know I could do it. It makes me feel . . . I don't know. Stronger. Confident. It's not easy to keep a position like this, but I've done it."

"I understand, Sweet," Lucky said slowly. "I truly do." Still, the constant striving, the shoving for power and position made his head spin. It had been bad enough taking Snap's place. How could Sweet bear the tension: always fighting to keep her status, always having to prove herself, day after day? He didn't let her see his shudder.

At least in Bella's Pack they were all equal. They might not be as efficient at survival as Sweet's Pack, but if he had to be in a Pack at all, Lucky thought Bella's way was the better one.

"I'm glad we met up again," he told Sweet awkwardly.

"So am I." She pricked an ear and watched him curiously.

Lucky scraped at the pebbles with his claws. "I think I'd like to go for a walk on my own now. Is that all right? If Alpha can do it . . ."

Sweet's eyes widened. "You can't do everything Alpha can do."

"A walk alone can't hurt the Pack."

"No." Her voice had grown harder and cooler again. "But just because you beat Snap, don't start thinking you can challenge Alpha's authority. That would be a different game altogether. Even Fiery couldn't defeat Alpha, if he was stupid enough to try."

Lucky bristled at her tone. "Fiery doesn't have enough ambition to challenge Alpha. That's all."

"Fiery's smart enough to stick to the rules. And you should be too." Standing, Sweet turned her haunches to him and began to pad back toward the camp. She paused only to glance back once more over her shoulder. "Remember what happened to Mulch."

Remember what happened to Mulch.

How could he forget?

Lucky stood staring at the space where Sweet had been for a long time after she vanished into the forest, but at last he turned back to the lake. It rippled so calmly, so peacefully, and the Moon-Dog trail still lay broad and bright on its surface. If the Moon-Dog was Alpha's special Spirit Dog, would she betray Lucky to the brutal dog-wolf? Or would Moon-Dog understand what he was about to do?

Lucky gave a high brief whimper of unhappiness into the night.

Remember what happened to Mulch. . . .

He couldn't go on like this. Sweet's last words had finally made up his mind. That she could do what she'd done to Mulch was bad enough—but to threaten Lucky with the same fate? He caught a whine gathering in the back of his throat and swallowed hard. *Stop that, Lucky!*

He was filled with a fierce longing to put as much distance as he could between himself and Alpha's Pack—between himself and his terrible guilt. For the sake of protecting his own hide, he'd done a terrible thing to Mulch, and all on the orders of that sneering little creature Whine.

After all, he'd found out everything Bella could possibly need to know. There was no reason for him to stay, none at all. Part of him knew that he had only stayed this long because he'd wanted to: because he was a hunter, a dog with status; because of the Great Howl. It was a part of himself he was afraid of. If he gave in to it, would he lose the rest of what made him Lucky?

Almost without realizing, he was already walking away. Along the edge of the waves he broke into a loping run, eager now to get far from Alpha's Pack, and as fast as he could. He would miss

Sweet, he couldn't deny that, but she was Alpha's partner, and would soon be his mate. She could not have made clearer where her loyalties lay. He would miss some of the others, too, he realized—Twitch and Snap especially. He remembered with a pang how he'd promised to teach Snap some City Dog tricks.

But I don't belong with Snap, or with Sweet, and I certainly don't belong with Alpha.

Do I?

The Moon-Dog was still high; Bella would be at the longpaw campsite. Urgency lent him speed and nimbleness, and he made his way swiftly through the darkly shadowed wood, feeling a nip of nervousness whenever the pale clear moonlight picked him out. His legs pumped beneath him. The thought of what he was doing drove him on; what if Bella left before he arrived? What if she wasn't there at all?

What if she's given up on me . . . ?

A great rush of relief hit him when he smelled the old-smoke reek that reminded him of the camp. He bounded into the clearing to see Bella there waiting for him. With a low bark of greeting, she trotted up and licked him as he stood panting.

She cocked her head, waiting patiently for him to catch his breath. "I'd almost given up on you, Yap. I was about to leave!"

He nuzzled her. "Don't give up on me, Squeak. Not yet!"

Her eyes were bright and happy, he noticed. "It's been a few no-suns since you met Daisy and Sunshine. What kept you?"

"I'm running out of excuses to slip away," he said, and sat down. Now that he could see her clearly in the pale light of the Moon-Dog, he noticed signs of tiredness in the creases around Bella's eyes. There were scratches on her nose, and a shallow gash on her left shoulder, but despite all that she seemed carefree. Almost triumphant . . . and there was something strange about her smell. Tentatively sniffing at her shoulder, he caught it distinctly: the scent of other animals, dark and musky.

A chill ran through his blood. Lucky took a step back from her. "Bella. What's going on?"

"We're all fine," Bella said brightly. "Your instructions about getting to the lake and the hunting grounds worked perfectly! I'm sure we'll be much stronger soon."

"Well . . . that's good, but it's not what I meant. You look hurt!"

Bella tossed her head dismissively. "Some Wild Dogs we had to fight off. But we managed!"

Lucky was speechless. Since when had his litter-sister happily fought battles with Wild Dogs, and won? And all while he was stuck in the Wild Pack, doing her tricky spy work. There was a rustle in the grass as a field mouse stole past—the sound only made the silence between them seem even more painful.

"What about you, Lucky?" Bella asked eventually. "What's happened since last time?"

She sounded so bright and curious, Lucky found himself telling her everything, even though he begrudged each word. He had the strongest sense, in the uneasy tingling of his fur, that she wasn't telling him the whole truth—yet she expected just that from him!

Bella was listening keenly, and gave a sharp little bark of encouragement as he paused. "And Daisy's already told me about your adventures with the giant loudcages—they sounded terrible!"

"They were. And it wasn't much of an adventure," he pointed out, miffed. "It was frightening, and if it hadn't been for Alpha—"

Bella's ears pricked sharply. She must have heard the respect in his voice when he was talking about the Pack leader. "What about him?"

"Never mind." He found he didn't want to explain his complicated feelings about Alpha—not to his litter-sister. "Anyway, that's what I've been dealing with, and those yellow-fur longpaws, too, while you've been fighting battles with Wild Dogs."

Her eyes were suddenly full of sympathy, and she nosed anxiously at his flank. "Were you hurt, Lucky?"

"No." *Thanks to Alpha.* "But, Bella, I've had enough. I want to come back, and we can move on together somewhere else. It's not just loudcages and longpaws—it's dangerous just being with that Pack. Omega—I mean Whine—could expose me at any moment. I'm not sure he's finished with me—and after the Moon-Dog's next turn, he'll be Omega again, I'm sure of it. That'll make him even more bitter and vengeful!"

"But that's a long time away!" barked Bella cheerfully. "You've kept that horrible dog happy for now. You'll be fine!"

Lucky stared at her. "That's not the point. It isn't just Whine! If those dogs ever find out I've betrayed them—well. You won't be seeing your litter-brother anymore. I'll be hunting worms with the Earth-Dog!"

Bella looked at her paws. "But you can't, Lucky. You can't come back."

His heart seemed to stop. "What do you mean?"

"Oh, Lucky, I don't mean forever. Just for now. You don't understand."

"No, I don't!" he barked angrily.

"Listen," Bella placated him. "Later, of course you can come back, Lucky. In a few days, perhaps! But Martha and Bruno are very unwell."

His gut turned over. "Still? Bella, this isn't right. They should be—"

"Oh, you mustn't worry, Lucky!" she said hurriedly. "You have enough to think about. It's a strange illness, that's all—their bellies ache all the time. I think the sickness might cling to food or water. Maybe even air! And it's creeping into other dogs' stomachs. That's all. They'll get better, but it would be silly for you to come back, and get sick. Wouldn't it?"

He stared at her for a long time. The nausea and disappointment were almost overwhelming, robbing him of his voice, and for a moment he felt his legs wobble and thought he'd have to lie down. *I still have to stay away?*

"I suppose . . . but . . ." Suddenly his disappointment turned into panic. "I put my life on the line for you and the Pack! I did everything you asked of me, I betrayed a dog, and now you're telling me I have to go back there?"

Bella quickly interrupted him. "While we're at such low strength, we still need you in the other camp. Do you see? We need you to spy for us a little longer, to keep the land safe for us to travel through, for food and water. It's best that you're . . . with them. You have to stay well, Lucky! We need you!"

She knows just where to nip me where it hurts, thought Lucky dismally. He gave a wretched whine.

"Please, Lucky? For me?"

Everything has been for you, Bella. "If I have to."

"Please, Lucky." Her eyes were dark and intent and solemn.

He shut his own, so that he wouldn't have to look at her. "Just a little longer, then. Only a little. Can I come back with you and see Martha and Bruno first? I'm worried about them."

Bella's tail drooped. "I wish you could," she said. "But I don't want you to catch this sickness."

Lucky slumped with disappointment. "You're right," he said sadly. "Tell them I'll be back as soon as I can."

"Thank you, Lucky." Bella nuzzled his ear. "Thank you."

"Bella, even going back tonight will be difficult. One of them—well, I think my absence might have been noticed." His gut twisted when he thought of how he'd left Sweet, and the things she'd said.

"Then you have to be careful, Yap." She licked him affectionately. "Don't get hurt. I don't want my litter-brother in any trouble."

Why not? It's you who got me into it! But in spite of his dread and misery, Lucky had to admit the sense in what she said. There was certainly no point in making himself ill, and it wouldn't be for much longer. Just till the sickness had worked its way out of her Pack, if it was as bad as she said it was. . . .

"Don't forget, then," he sighed. "Whine's a patrol dog now, and he's weak. And however cunning he is, he's not too competent as a Pack Dog. That's a soft spot you can exploit when you need to move around. And remember, the Wild Pack hunts late after sun-high. The meadows on this side of the forest have good hunting. If you do it in the early sunup, and avoid scent-marking, your presence should have faded enough by the time we come around."

"Yes, yes. I understand all that, Lucky." Bella seemed thoughtful and serious, but there was a hint of impatience in her tensed muscles, too. "Now you'd best be getting back, if you're worried. Be careful. And I promise you can be back with our Pack. Soon! It'll be before another turn of the Moon-Dog, I'm sure of it. Go on!" She licked his nose fondly, her tail wagging.

"Good-bye, then?"

"Good-bye, Lucky! May the Forest-Dog be with you!"

She'd dismissed him like a pup, he thought, as he loped back in the direction of the Wild Pack camp. *She wanted me gone. She couldn't wait for me to leave.* The very thought sent a chill of dread down his spine.

Don't be silly, Lucky! You're both anxious.

Still, he could feel his litter-sister watching him until he was well out of sight. The low-burning resentment in his belly was bad enough without this tingle of apprehension, too.

There was something Bella wasn't telling him.

He couldn't place his paw on it, but he knew it for sure. Something was horribly, dangerously wrong.

CHAPTER NINETEEN

The next day, Lucky sniffed carefully at each patch of grass among the gopher burrows, and even licked at tree stumps, but there was no trace of Bella or the other Leashed Dogs. Had they covered their tracks so well, and moved like ghosts as they hunted? Or had she ignored his advice and stayed away from the hunting meadows?

There was nothing about her he could be sure of anymore, he thought with a ripple of sadness and unease.

"Have you turned into a grass-eater?" Snap's cheerful bark made him jump. "Come on. There are rabbits!"

Snap was in a fine mood this afternoon, skittish and eager, and strangely enough her enthusiasm was catching. Lucky gave her a happy bark, suddenly glad to be jolted out of his misery.

"Drive a few my way and we'll see who's a grass-eater!"

Snap yelped a laugh and darted off, veering across the sun-splashed grassland until she disappeared beyond a rise in the ground. Only moments later panicked rabbits were careening toward him, and Lucky leaped after them with a gleeful bark. The creatures were in chaos, tumbling and racing across one another's paths to reach their burrows, and some were too mindless with fear to even try to avoid him. One furry streak bolted almost between Lucky's legs, but instead of doubling back he sprang for its companion, rolling the terrified rabbit over and over until he could grab its neck in his jaws and snap it.

The others were having just as much success. Out of the corner of his eye he saw Fiery shaking the life out of a rabbit with his powerful jaws, and Spring was playing with another almost like a well-fed sharpclaw. She tossed it into the air and caught it.

"Good hunting today!" she yelped as she slapped her rabbit to the ground with a deadly paw.

Lucky barked his agreement and turned to chase another before they could all vanish underground. He was so charged with the thrill of the hunt, his blood fizzing in his ears, that he didn't hear the first sharp barks of alarm.

It was Snap's wild cry that finally made him look up, letting another rabbit scamper free and down into its hole. Snap wasn't hunting anymore; she was staring at a dog who was racing across the meadow toward them, panting with distress.

"Dart?" she barked.

Fiery and Spring had frozen now, too, staring at the brown-and-white dog as she skidded to a halt.

"The camp!" Dart barked, breathless. "Come fast! The camp's under attack!"

"What?" snarled Fiery, and then: "My pups!"

"Dart, who? Who's attacking?" Spring bounded toward her, dropping a squealing gopher that skittered away as fast as it could.

"That Leashed Pack! There are more of them! And they're attacking us!"

No! Lucky thought, his brain in turmoil. *No, Bella! What have you done?*

"That's not possible—" began Snap.

"Yes! They sneaked past that slug-brain Whine! I knew he'd be a useless guard! They must have known the hunters were gone, and they're going to kill us!" Dart turned and bolted back the way she'd come.

Without another word, the hunters raced across the meadow after Dart, Lucky at Fiery's heels. He kept up with the furious pace though his heart was a stone inside him.

Branches whipped Lucky's muzzle as they plunged into the trees, but all he could see was Fiery's brown haunches as he pounded through the flickering sun-shadows. He didn't dare think. His Packmates were a blur of speed at his sides. *Packmates.* Lucky's belly twisted with guilt.

They were out of the trees and into the clearing before he could stop his brain from spinning. Lucky scrabbled to a halt beside Fiery as the huge dog squared up to the invaders, snarling and bristling.

The scene in the camp made Lucky's stomach turn over. His Pack, the dogs he'd guided and protected and spied for, facing up against—

My other Pack, he realized with a jolt.

Bella was clearly in the lead, her tail stiff and her hackles high as she grimly faced down Alpha. Daisy and Sunshine were both trembling, but they stood firm, small teeth bared. Mickey was beside them, looking determined and fierce.

And there were two others.

Bruno. Martha.

The sturdy dog and the massive water-dog looked sleek and healthy and ready for a battle, not a sign of sickness in their eyes or their coats. Martha wasn't even limping anymore. *Bella lied to me . . .*

They all lied to me!

Lucky watched as the two Packs circled each other warily,

growling and tense, each waiting for the first sign of weakness in the other.

Every hair on Lucky's body was erect, and tremors of tension ran through his skin and muscles, but there was nothing he could do. He couldn't even move, and though his mind raced in frantic circles like a rabbit, he couldn't come up with a single useful thought. Where did he fit in this stupid, dangerous situation?

Whose side are you on, Lucky?

For a moment, his resentment and bewilderment made him dizzy. Why hadn't Bella told him this was what she was planning? Did she not trust him, or had she wanted to make him some kind of unwitting bait? And what in the name of the Sky-Dogs made her think this could work? Alpha's Pack was still bigger and fiercer than hers.

I can't stand by while my litter-sister fights for her life. . . .

Can I?

"Get *out*, longpaw pets!" Sweet barked. "We'll destroy you for this."

"We'll go where we want to," Bruno snarled.

"And that includes the lake, and the hunting meadows," growled Mickey. "If you don't like it, by all means try to fight us."

Twitch made a feinting move forward, but still none of the

dogs launched a proper attack. Alpha's eyes were cold and deadly, riveted on Bella's, and Lucky knew that if any dog was going to die that day it would be her.

But he feared there would be more than one going to the Earth-Dog, before the Sun-Dog lay down to rest. Many more . . .

Maybe I can still talk them all down from this.

No. It's hopeless. Oh, Forest-Dog, help me. I don't know what to do!

The dog-smells around him were sharp and rank: anger and hatred and fear. The air was thick with it, but there was something else, something that made him sniff the breeze. None of the others had noticed, too concerned with threatening one another. Snarling and whining filled the glade, making his ears ache, but there was nothing wrong with his nose.

I know that scent.

Frantically Lucky opened his nostrils and snuffed the air, desperate to pinpoint the elusive odor. It was familiar somehow . . . and then he knew why. He'd smelled it on Bella at their last meeting—that dark, dusky scent he couldn't place.

Bella had said it was dogs they'd fought off. Had she lied about that, too? Had she brought them as hidden reinforcements? Or had they returned to have their revenge on her; were they even now waiting beyond the trees?

A great courageous bark silenced the low growls of challenge. Bella.

"Alpha!" she cried. "We're here to demand a share of this territory. You have food, water, shelter. Share it, or we'll take it by force!"

Lucky stared at her, open-jawed. Had she lost her mind?

Alpha clearly thought so. "You're welcome to try," he told her in his silky growl. He shared an amused glance with Sweet before turning back to Bella. "If you're stupid enough to take us on. But if you're smarter than I take you for, you'll leave now. And then," he licked a huge paw idly, making the long claws gleam, "we'll say no more about it."

Lucky doubted it would be that easy, but still he barked at Bella inside his head. *Slink away now, Bella, while you have the chance!*

She didn't even blink or cower. Instead she drew herself even stiffer and higher, and said, "You're making a huge mistake, Alpha."

For the first time the dog-wolf looked genuinely surprised, his ears pricking forward in disbelief. Then he gave a great bark of laughter. "I'm not the one making a mistake, Leashed Dog. Not me!"

Bella said nothing, only wrinkling her muzzle in disdain. Then she gave a great summoning bark.

Shadows rippled through the bushes; pointed snouts lined with gleaming teeth emerged from all around. Lucky felt a roiling dread in his belly. The other dogs of the Wild Pack were glancing around nervously, showing the whites of their eyes. From all around, creatures were creeping slyly into view. . . .

Foxes!

In sheer disbelief, Lucky watched them, gray and thin and savage. One snapped its cruel teeth, its tail standing up straight.

"With you, Bella-dog," it leered. "Hello, smelly-dogs."

Lucky's head reeled and his stomach churned. So that was the reek on Bella's fur, the scent he couldn't quite identify. Not dogs at all. And not Bella's enemies—they were with her!

"Foxes!" howled Alpha in rage. "Foxes in my lair!"

The dogs around him erupted into a din of furious yelping as Lucky backed away, horrified. Foxes were creatures of the city, feral and wily and savage. Why had they come here? They belonged in the broken longpaw town, scavenging and lurking and killing by stealth. How in the name of the Sky-Dogs had Bella found them, and why?

Did she go back to the city? For these?

A great hideous shudder went through his bones. *What has she promised them?*

"I told you you were making a mistake." Bella's growl was cool and certain. "We're not weak Leashed Dogs now, Alpha, and you can't drive us from this valley."

Alpha stood stock-still in disgust, rigid and stunned.

"My friends," barked Bella. "Attack!"

CHAPTER TWENTY

"NO!"

But Lucky's howl of protest was drowned out by the deafening barks and screams of dogs colliding in battle. Bella had knocked Sweet flying, but Sweet was already on her paws again, snarling her rage as she tore at Bella's neck. Mickey and Bruno were taking on Snap and Spring, and they rolled on the crushed grass and earth, snapping and biting and scratching. Yelps of pain and fury battered Lucky's ears as he saw the foxes spring like streaks of gray mist at the Wild Pack, tearing and raking at their ears and eyes and throats.

His heart was pounding so hard it felt too big for his chest. *Oh, help me, Forest-Dog! I don't know what to do!* He didn't want to see the Leashed Dogs defeated and killed, but how could he fight against his comrades in the Wild Pack? How could he ally himself with foxes? They weren't to be trusted, ever!

His whole body was shaking with the struggle to choose, but

if he didn't get involved soon, one or the other of his Packs would start to fail. His friends would be killed. He didn't want any of them to die! The foxes could go to the Earth-Dog as far as he was concerned, but not the dogs he knew, the ones he fought and hunted beside—

The foxes . . .

Lucky crouched, creeping forward, peering into the pitching, tumbling bodies as they fought and howled. All dogs, though—all dogs, killing one another. Where were the foxes?

He sprang to his paws and spun around. Six gray shapes were scuttling around the food store, grabbing any scraps they could. *Treacherous brutes!* Lucky almost felt sorry for Bella, with her trusting innocence. He'd been wrong about these animals—they weren't city foxes at all. They were too ruthless and cunning. Foxes living off scraps in the city would look slow and lazy by comparison.

He snarled and bolted after the thieves. The foxes wouldn't get even a scrap if he had anything to do with it.

As he ran, the sickening realization hit him like a longpaw's kick. The foxes had lost interest in the meager food store, and had come to circle Moon's den. They paced around it, their eyes fixed on the pups, lips curled back in snarls. They didn't want scraps,

Lucky thought with a flash of pure rage. They wanted prey, live prey. Moon's pups.

Moon was crouched before the den, snarling her hate, spittle flying from her jaws as the foxes darted in one by one to bite and torment her.

"Mommy-dog, tired, all alone," Lucky heard one of them say. "Can't fight our hunger!"

Moon was weak from nursing, but she was as fierce as Alpha ever had been, clawing and snapping at her tormentors. Squirm, Fuzz, and Nose were cowering somewhere behind her, and Lucky could hear their terrified whimpering.

Lucky cannoned into the middle of the fox-pack, sending them scattering and rolling onto their backs, but his surprise attack gave Moon only a short reprieve. The foxes bounced back to their paws, flying at him.

All of Lucky's fury poured through him as he leaped and snapped and drew fox blood, flinging one away as the next came at him. This was a fight he could throw himself into without doubts or torn loyalties. Moon's eyes met his with a flash of gratitude, and she turned on the foxes with new hope and energy, fighting as hard as she could from her post at the den's mouth. The foxes were clever fighters, taunting and nipping her, trying to draw her away from the den.

"Give us tasty pup-snacks!" one of the foxes whined.

Lucky heard the pups howling in terror. "No, Mother, don't go!"

"Don't leave us!"

Moon looked exhausted, but she battled on.

A fox sprang onto her neck, snatching a mouthful of skin and hanging on. Lucky snarled and struck his own attacker across the snout with a paw, then dashed for Moon, seizing the fox and tearing it from her. Yelping with agony, Moon rolled away. At the same time, Lucky felt sharp fangs sink into his flank, and he had to turn to crunch his jaws into the fox that had grabbed him.

Are these creatures unkillable? he thought in despair as it tumbled over in the grass, then came back at him, drool and blood flying from its muzzle.

They were so strong, so resilient—much hardier brutes than the ones he used to fight in the city, and worst of all, braver. Any of the foxes of the city would have run from him by now.

He snapped at one that was sneaking to his flank, but suddenly there were two more. They came at him from both sides, biting his neck fur and holding on hard. Lucky felt the warm flow of blood and the sting of pain, dazing him and making his head spin. They were dragging him, but he didn't know for a moment which way was up and which way was down. He was falling, rolling, over and over—

His skull cracked against a rock, and suddenly, horribly, he couldn't see. The world was a blur, swimming before his eyes as if he were underwater. Trying to stand, he found his legs wouldn't work.

Moon! She's alone!

He dug his claws into the earth and dragged himself toward the courageous Mother-Dog, but there was blood in his eyes now. He could see her still fighting, raking at the attacking foxes, but there were too many of them. Too many . . .

Something gray was slinking past Moon's back legs as she defended her shoulder. Lucky tried to bark a warning, but the sound was feeble; maybe he hadn't managed to make it at all. The next thing in his vision was that gray thing again, crawling from Moon's den with a small bundle of wriggling black-and-white in its jaws. A mewling, terrified pup . . .

Two high voices seemed to echo through his mind. "No, Fuzz, no!"

With a last surge of energy, Lucky struggled to his feet, swaying. The world whirled around him.

What was that? Among the trees!

Oh, he was imagining things now. His head wound must have flung him into a dream. He couldn't help Moon from a dream.

Lucky blinked blood furiously from his eyes, staggering. No, there were forest-shadows. He couldn't have imagined them.

There. Big ghosts in the woods, sleek and strong ghosts: not moving, just watching. Two great black-and-tan Fierce Dogs, still as stone, eyes burning. *Dogs! Why don't they help us? Why don't they move?* One of the dogs turned its head away. The other raised a paw, as if it might finally step out of the shadows. Lucky stumbled forward, then jerked his head up again. *No. Lucky, you fool! There were no dogs; it was a dream. There were no shadows in the trees....*

Get away, dream dogs. This was what was real, this turmoil of blood and struggle and fear. Moon was defending her pups to the death, and he had to get to her.

He staggered forward. Two of them, and the helpless pups. Him and Moon, and six savage foxes.

If I have to die, I'll take the Earth-Dog a gift—of foxes. Lucky opened his jaws in a howl of defiance and sprang.

CHAPTER TWENTY-ONE

As the leader fox turned on him with bared fangs, Lucky snarled his furious challenge.

"I won't go easily," he warned them. "If you try to kill me, I'll take you with . . ." But before he could finish, a blow knocked him sideways into the grass. Lucky yelped in shock, shaking his head violently.

Not a fox. A great brown shape hurtled past him, all muscle and fury and slavering jaws. Fiery!

Fiery landed among the foxes like a great falling tree, sending them yelping and flying onto their backs. Seizing a straggler, he flung it aside and lunged at another. Lucky, still woozy from the blow to his head, felt his heart swell with new courage. Struggling back to his paws, he plunged in alongside Fiery, fighting the foxes fiercely. He let loose a volley of barks, hoping it would alert some of the other dogs who still battled among themselves at the other side of the clearing, oblivious to the foxes' treachery.

Only two of them must have heard, but they came racing at once—Mulch, his black ears flying, and Daisy, a small ball of teeth and fierceness.

"Help Moon!" Lucky had time to yelp before he was attacked once more, a fox darting in to sink its sharp teeth into his hind leg.

The pain was like a scorch of flame, but it finally cleared his head. Lucky snarled and bit, tossing the fox away.

From the corner of his eye he saw another fox slash viciously at Daisy, its claw slicing a line of blood across her muzzle. But she rallied, her eyes flashing; she sank her sharp little teeth deep into its throat, hanging on fiercely until it stopped moving.

Lucky dodged as another fox threw itself at him, then pounced on it, clamping its leg between his jaws.

"Out of the way, stink-dog!" one of the foxes shrieked. Lucky looked up and saw three foxes pouncing on Mulch. The black dog vanished under a pile of scratching, gnawing fury. Lucky saw Mulch kick helplessly at his attackers, blood drops scattering.

"Mulch! Hang on!" Fiery barked, a single swipe of his massive paw scattering the two foxes that were trying to take him down.

Panting, free of attackers just for a few moments, Lucky stood stiff-legged and barked, high and desperate.

"Alpha! Sweet! Bella! Help!"

At last, at last, his cries were heard. Across the clearing, dogs stumbled apart, shaking themselves, momentarily stunned. They all seemed to realize in the same moment what had happened. Alpha gave a high howl of fury, and plunged forward; behind him, like a single Pack, the rest of the dogs hurtled across toward Moon's den.

Lucky was too busy tearing the three foxes from Mulch's prone body to see the end of the struggle. He was only dimly aware of the onrush of the dogs, the yelps of the retreating foxes. One by one Mulch's attackers fell away, scrambling off him and dashing to defend themselves, but Alpha and Sweet were moving among them now like Lightning, slashing and springing with deadly efficiency. Tails between their legs, the foxes fell over one another in their frantic bids to escape.

"Run time!" they called to one another. "Out, out, out!"

Silence, when it came, seemed very sudden. Lucky stood with his head hanging down, tongue lolling and flanks heaving. Three thin, gray fox-shapes were racing away into the undergrowth; the other three lay broken and battered on the churned, bloody earth.

The leader-fox's voice cried shrilly into the eerily still air. "Be back! We come back, filthy dogs. For your other pup-prey!"

Then he was gone, and only the breeze stirred the bushes.

Grimly, Alpha lifted a limp fox-corpse into the air with his jaws and tossed it away from him. It thudded to the ground close to where Mulch lay.

As if their leader had broken some awful spell, Fiery let out a great baying howl of distress, and Moon lay down, whining with grief and shock. As two small bodies wriggled fearfully from the den behind her, she and Fiery curled protectively around their surviving pups, and Moon licked feverishly at their tiny heads.

Lucky couldn't bear to watch them. "Daisy!" he barked gruffly. "Are you all right?"

The little dog shook herself, rubbing her muzzle against a patch of soft grass. "I'm fine, Lucky. It's a scratch. Quick, it's the black dog you should look after." Daisy turned her nose unhappily toward Mulch. "He's much worse."

Together with the others of the Wild Pack, Lucky limped across to Mulch, who lay in a pool of thickening blood.

Pain jolted through his wounded leg, but that wasn't what made him stop after a few paces. There was no need to go to Mulch. Flies were already settling on his wounded side, and the scent drifting from him was bitterly familiar.

Like Alfie . . .

"He's gone to the Earth-Dog," came Alpha's growl. "Leave him."

"No," murmured Lucky, feeling despair take over.

"Leave him, I said! Mulch fought bravely, but he's gone."

The sound of Mulch's proper name coming from Alpha's jaws stunned Lucky, and he sat down heavily on his haunches. The leader hadn't called him Omega. In death, Mulch had regained his status and his dignity.

The things Lucky had taken from him.

The black wave of misery that swept over him was worse than anything Lucky had felt before, in all his deceptions and double-dealing. Guilt and shame coiled around his heart and guts like a snake, crushing his innards. The pain was wrenching, so much worse than the gash in his leg.

I brought it on myself. And I brought this all upon the Pack.

He couldn't contain the feeling inside him; it wasn't possible. Lifting his head, Lucky let out a great echoing howl of grief and agony.

Snap turned to him, shocked, but she sat down and raised her muzzle to howl with him. Then Twitch was howling too, and Dart, and suddenly Martha and Bruno and Daisy were joining in. In moments all the dogs were howling to the sky, united in mourning.

No Spirit Dogs bounded across Lucky's vision now. *They've*

deserted me, he thought, *and so they should.* His voice broke, his howl faltered, and Snap stopped too, to lick his ear comfortingly.

"It wasn't your fault," she said.

"No," added Spring, at his flank. "You did all you could, Lucky."

"You fought for Moon's pups," added Dart. "Mulch came to help you, and he died bravely."

As the three of them resumed their mournful cries, Lucky found himself voiceless. He sat among the grieving dogs, their howls tearing through his heart. Whine was watching him very intently, but he found he didn't care about that sly little brute anymore.

I did all I could, he thought bitterly. *I betrayed my friends, and brought Bella and the foxes here, and destroyed Mulch. And Fuzz.*

If the Earth-Dog opened her jaws to swallow him now, Lucky thought savagely, he'd go willingly. Without so much as a whimper.

CHAPTER TWENTY-TWO

The Packs were subdued as they cleared the camp of bodies. They dragged the three foxes out to the hunting meadow for the crows. Martha used her giant, webbed feet to push their bodies across the ground while Daisy did her best to help, despite the injury on her muzzle. *She fought well,* Lucky thought, watching her.

Over them all lay a sense of dread; Lucky could feel it like a wet slab of mud-slip. This wasn't finished; there were things still to be done and said that were only waiting out of respect for the dead. Lucky didn't dare look at Alpha, or even at Sweet; and he couldn't bring himself to glance at his litter-sister. He had betrayed the Wild Pack for Bella, and she had given him nothing but lies.

For all the vicious fighting, no one had won, and they all knew it. The sense of doom and despair weighed in his belly like a great stone, and he knew he couldn't bear the guilt he carried for long.

The Wild Pack turned to their own dead, gently moving

Mulch's and Fuzz's bodies down under a brightly flowering bush just outside the camp.

Sweet turned and pressed her muzzle to Moon's neck. "There's no time for a long good-bye right now. I promise we'll mourn them properly."

The realization that he didn't know how the Wild Pack honored their dead stung Lucky like a fox bite. He would fight to the end for these dogs, but he still wasn't one of them—not really. Not yet.

Fiery and Moon crouched together beside the bush for a second, with Squirm and Nose trembling between them. Then they got up and walked away.

"Now let us settle this," barked Alpha from his rock. "Both Packs, to me." Lucky was almost relieved. At last his fate would be clear.

Some of the dogs trotted eagerly to the circle, keen to see matters resolved between the Packs; others, like Lucky and Bella, limped there, whether hurt or filled with dread. Alpha waited till all the dogs had gathered, then gazed around them with his cold, unsettling eyes. Sweet, at his side, looked almost as fierce and unforgiving as he did.

"You," growled Alpha, turning to Bella. "Leashed fool."

Despite everything, Lucky couldn't help but admire his litter-sister's staunchly defiant stance. As she stepped forward she looked Alpha full in his yellow eyes, her head proud.

"You brought foxes into my camp," growled the dog-wolf, "and death to my Pack. If you want to speak before you die, do it now."

The other dogs stirred uneasily, the Leashed Dogs whining and barking in protest, and Lucky's fur prickled. Sunshine whimpered softly and Bruno's brow creased in deep folds of anxiety. Lucky had been afraid of this; only Bella could save herself now.

"You denied us hunting and fresh water," she told Alpha fearlessly. "We had no choice. If you'd listened to reason from the start, none of this would have happened. And you killed one of us!"

Alpha gave a belly-deep bark of anger. "You've had your vengeance for that, haven't you? I wonder if it will be worth it." The light in his yellow eyes was as dangerous as fire. "You Leashed Dogs invaded my territory. You had no right under the Law of Dogs— none. Unless you were willing to fight for it, and you couldn't even do that until you'd made allies of those . . . vermin."

Bella dropped her eyes. "The foxes lied to me," she said softly. "I was wrong to bring them here, and I'm sorry."

"You'll be even more sorry." Alpha curled his muzzle. "I'll kill you myself."

"No!" barked Sunshine, and Alpha turned to her, crushing her with his fierce glare. "Please don't," she whimpered more humbly. "Please. Bella's a good dog."

"A good leader," put in Bruno. He threw Lucky a glance as if to say: *Tell them!*

But Lucky didn't have the chance. The Alpha shook his head. "A good leader would have thought ahead. She put you in as much peril as she put my Pack, and it's only our bad luck that none of you died. It's time to rectify that. Bella of the Leashed Pack, come here."

"Alpha, wait." Moon paced forward, leaving her two remaining pups between Fiery's protective paws. "May I say something?"

Every dog in the circle looked at her in surprise, but none more than Alpha. He licked his chops thoughtfully. "You of all dogs here have a right to speak, Moon. What is it?"

Moon turned, studying each dog in the circle very carefully. At last she tilted her head directly at Alpha, her gaze forthright.

"I lost a pup today because of these Leashed Dogs and their foolish leader," she began.

Lucky's heart fell. If Moon spoke against her, Bella truly was doomed.

"I have as much reason to hate them as you do, Alpha. More." Moon's ear twitched, and she shivered a little, then recovered, her voice strengthening. "But Bella told the truth. It's obvious the foxes duped her; she never intended this to happen the way it did. That's stupidity, Alpha, not wickedness."

Alpha nodded. "That may be, but she may still deserve to die. I think you have more to say, Moon. Tell us."

"We've all done foolish things. We've all made mistakes. And we'll make many more in the days to come. Look how the world has changed!" Moon scraped the earth with her paw. "Who's to say who will make the next deadly error? We need to stick together, live together. It's hard enough for dogs to survive in the world of the Big Growl without turning on one another."

Alpha gave a reluctant nod, but his voice remained stern and hard. "They also have to act properly. Respect the Law of Dogs."

"I haven't finished." Moon closed her eyes. "They brought the foxes here; it's true. But when they knew they'd made a mistake, they did their best to make it right. Three of my pups would have died today if not for Lucky and poor Mulch . . . and for this Leashed Dog."

Moon turned her head to gaze at Daisy. The little dog's eyes were wide and awestruck, and she trembled a little, but didn't move.

"This Daisy came to my pups' aid when Lucky called her, and fought like a warrior for their sake." Lucky listened even harder as Moon continued. "And when they heard, so did the rest of her Pack. That means, in my eyes, they are forgiven. I still have two pups I might not have had."

Moon lay down, her paws in front of her, as if she was too weary to say more. But Fiery licked Squirm's and Nose's little heads, settling them where they were, and lumbered forward to her side.

"I agree with Moon," he growled. "It was our pup who died, but it was our other two pups who were saved. The Leashed Dogs were wrong to do what they did, but they did the right thing in the end. That shows courage and honor, Alpha, and I respect it."

Fiery's tail lashed slowly as he bent down to nuzzle Moon's head. The other dogs stood in hushed silence, watching Alpha as he scowled down at the two mates. There was fondness in his frown, though, and Lucky found his hopes rising just a little.

"Beta. Do your job." Alpha sighed and glanced at his elegant partner. "Advise me."

Sweet scratched thoughtfully at her ear, then placed her paw gracefully back on the rock. "It's true that they fought well," she murmured. "Whether against us or for us."

"And which of those carries most weight?" asked Alpha.

Sweet made a rumbling sound in her throat. "They would be worthy allies, and bad enemies. I suggest we put aside our differences with the Leashed Pack, Alpha. There's more that draws us together than divides us. As Moon said, we are all dogs, and we're living in a changed world. When I came here after the first Big Growl, I thought this Pack was safe from its effects, but I nearly died in the second Growl, and who knows what else is to come?"

"And their leader?" Alpha's baleful gaze rested on Bella once more.

"Hmph." Sweet gave her a cutting look. "I'm willing to do what Moon and Fiery want. It seems to me they have the right to decide."

Alpha licked his jaws again thoughtfully, his pointed white teeth gleaming.

"Very well," he said at last. "Beta talks sense yet again, and she also talks me out of my instincts. Again. How shall we arrange this new order?"

Sweet sat down, eyeing the members of Bella's Pack. "I suggest we invite their Pack to join with ours. But every one of them will have to accept a low place in the hierarchy. They must be loyal only to you. If they're willing to do that, it'll prove we can work together for the good of all."

Alpha nodded as Bella's Pack exchanged nervous but hopeful glances. Lucky stared at the ground, torn. Could Bella's Pack really fit in with these true Wild Dogs? He shuddered to imagine Sunshine in the hierarchy, trying to find a place for herself that was survivable. How did he feel about the Packs uniting?

Bad, was the answer. And good. And everything in between. Lucky shut his eyes in despair.

He blinked them open when Alpha scraped his claws against the rock, a screeching sound against the stillness of the clearing.

"Very well. We'll organize the Pack roles as best we can, if the Leashed Dogs agree to join us. Which they will, if they have any sense. We still won't tolerate outsiders trespassing on our land, so they will join us or run far away."

"And their leader?" prompted Sweet.

"She will be Omega," growled Alpha. "Do you know what that means, pet dogs? She will fetch and carry for the Pack, take *all* orders without complaining, and if she has any time to sleep she'll be in the Omega den, drafty and damp. That can be justice for Mulch. When a full turn of the Moon-Dog has passed, she can challenge if she likes. If she survives that long."

Bella stood up, her hackles raising. Lucky's fur shivered. Was she deciding whether to fight after all? Around her, her Pack muttered and whined.

"Don't do anything you're not comfortable with," said Martha.

Bruno growled: "Show them you can survive!"

Lucky longed suddenly to be one of them, to be able to guide and advise them like he used to. Becoming Omega for a turn of the Moon-Dog was Bella's best hope, he knew. Surely she did, too? But he couldn't interfere. He didn't dare.

I'm not one of them. Not openly. Not if I want to live. . . .

This whole battle, everything that had happened, was his fault. He'd agreed to Bella's suggestion of becoming a spy, not thinking for a moment that she would deceive him. Worse, he'd told Bella about Whine and what a poor patrol dog he'd be; he'd given her the information about when the hunters would be away from the camp. All his spying hadn't helped Bella and her Pack; all it had done was harm all the dogs, and in the most horrible way. When Bella and her friends made their choice, what would he do?

Will I remain with a larger Pack? Or if they stay separate, will I stick with Bella, or find a new place here with the Wild Pack?

Or will I do what I always meant to do, and strike off alone again?

Bella and Alpha were still staring each other down, but Bella was licking her chops nervously now. At any moment she'd make her choice.

"Well?" sneered Alpha. "The decision's yours, Bella the Leashed Dog."

"Wait," barked a new voice.

Lucky took a breath, startled. As all the dogs turned, the pudgy dog who'd gotten Lucky into this mess trotted forward, head and tail high, an expression of cocky vindictiveness on his snub-nosed face.

"Don't decide anything yet, Alpha." Whine sat down, tilting his head at Lucky.

Sweet snapped her teeth at him. "Who are you to interfere, Whine? If Bella rejects our offer you'll be back to Omega, and don't you forget it."

"Oh, but I have something interesting to tell you." Whine's tongue lolled as his mouth stretched in a wide grin. "Alpha needs to know this, before he takes any new dogs into our Pack. You see that City Dog?"

Alpha glanced at Lucky, irritated, and back at Whine. "What about him?"

Lucky's heart was frozen in his chest. Nowhere to run, nowhere to hide. Whine was watching him closely, licking his teeth. Lucky felt himself shrink, his forequarters ready to bow, ready to beg uselessly for mercy.

"He's one of them. One of the Leashed Pack." Whine gave a bark of angry excitement. "He's been spying for them all along!"

Silence. Lucky's tongue felt thick and unwieldy in his jaws, and his coat prickled all over with icy fear. Bella's friends watched him with horror, giving him away just by their aghast expressions. The Wild Pack were all turning to him, one by one, their shock and disbelief plain.

Sweet bounded an abrupt pace forward, swinging a paw across Whine's face. He squealed, but didn't back off.

"That isn't true!" she barked angrily. "You'll take a beating for that lie, Omega."

"Stop!" barked Lucky, lunging forward between Sweet and Whine. His jaws opened as he panted for breath. Terror filled him, but he couldn't let yet another dog suffer for his misdeeds. Not even Whine.

"Lucky?" Sweet sounded bewildered.

"It's true." Lucky lowered his head, then jerked it up again to look her in the eyes. He owed her that, while he told her the truth. "He isn't lying, Sweet. What he says is true."

Sweet's eyes were wide and hurt, disbelieving. "No!"

"Yes. Sweet, I'm so sorry. I never meant for it to go this far. I . . . I wanted to belong here too."

She stared at him in silence for moments that seemed like days. Behind her, Alpha was ominously still.

Sweet's throat sounded tight. "You couldn't . . . You *wouldn't* . . ."

"Yes, Sweet. I did. I'm sorry."

"But you're one of us now," Sweet barked suddenly. "Even if it is true, you're . . ." She broke off and slammed her jaws shut.

Lucky opened his jaws. There was so much in her eyes: anger, hurt, fear, betrayal. A plea for him to say what she wanted him to say.`

Lucky swung around to look at Alpha, and then at Bella. Glancing at the other dogs in the circle, he caught sight of Whine's smug scowl, and Snap's bewilderment, and Fiery's gruff challenge. Daisy and Sunshine were trembling. He could smell the tension in the air, sense the raising of hairs and the racing of blood.

Time to choose, Lucky. Time to choose where your loyalties lie.

Then the great dog-wolf paced forward toward him, and Lucky stood to meet him, shaking.

Perhaps there was no choice for him to make at all.

Perhaps it was only time to die.

SURVIVORS

BOOK 3:
DARKNESS FALLS

After a violent attack threatened both the Wild and Leashed Packs, Lucky knows that the dogs' only hope for survival is to unite. The Wild Pack's ruthless Alpha reluctantly agrees to let Bella and the Leashed Dogs join them—but after learning of Lucky's role as a spy, Alpha casts Lucky out. And Lucky soon discovers that the forest and ruined city are treacherous for a Lone Dog . . .

CHAPTER ONE

Lucky froze, his legs trembling. Silence fell over the circle of dogs.

Alpha's broad, wolfish face was unreadable. He drew himself up on his rock, towering over the two Packs. By his side on the grass was Sweet, the beautiful swift-dog, staring at Lucky. Lucky could scarcely look at her.

Little snub-nosed Whine's tongue lolled and his jaws gaped. "You see, I was right! The City Dog was spying for the Leashed Dogs. He met with that one, the one who looks like him!" Whine turned to Bella, who glared until he cringed and cowered. "I saw them . . ." The little dog's words trailed off.

Lucky fought to keep his tail high. He could not let it droop in submission. That would show weakness—it would be the end of him in the eyes of this fierce Wild Pack.

They were all waiting for an explanation, but what could he say? He had spied on them, just as Whine had said. He had never imagined, though, that Bella would use the information he'd provided to attack the Wild Pack's camp.

Lucky searched the faces of the dogs in the circle.

What do I do now? If I show loyalty to the Leashed Pack, the others will kill me. But how can I turn my back on the Leashed Dogs? Bella's my litter-sister. . . .

He had been through so much with the Leashed Dogs. But the Wild Pack had accepted him as one of their own. He had shared the Great Howl with them, where Spirit Dogs ran before his eyes. He had felt the power of their bond, even as he balked at Alpha's strict hierarchy.

Then there was Sweet. . . . He stole a glance in her direction and she met his eye. He saw pain and confusion there, but also hope.

She raised her muzzle. "Lucky fought bravely to defend the pups from the foxes. Whatever he may have done before . . . he's no *Leashed* Dog. He's one of our Pack now." Her velvety ears twitched and she looked away. Her voice was uncertain, despite her words.

It's as though she wants to believe it, thought Lucky. *She wants to believe that I'm who she thought I was. . . .*

Lucky barked gratefully, even though he wasn't sure *where* he belonged.

He looked at his litter-sister. Bella stared hard at him, head slightly cocked.

She knows it's true. A part of me has grown loyal to the Wild Pack.

For a moment he felt guilty. Then he reminded himself that it was because of Bella that he had joined the Wild Dogs in the first place! And it was she who had brought the foxes into their home! She must have been crazy to trust those wily creatures. They'd betrayed her as soon as she'd led them to the camp, attacking Moon and threatening to eat her pups. He remembered how dogs from both Packs had broken off their battle to defend the pups when the foxes attacked them—first Daisy and Mulch, then the others. They had come together, repelling the vicious foxes. They had worked as a single, powerful Pack. . . .

Lucky noticed Moon and Fiery standing a few paces behind the others, their pups Squirm and Nose—the ones who had survived—nuzzled between them. Lucky's chest tightened with sorrow when he remembered the terror and turmoil, the frenzied barking, and the dogs who hadn't made it: little, helpless Fuzz, and poor Mulch.

Alpha growled low in his throat. "Lucky may have served our Pack for a time, but that does not excuse his treachery. What do you have to say for yourself, *City* Dog?"

Lucky licked his leg where a fox had mauled it, playing for time. His quick thinking rarely let him down, but this time he couldn't find anything to say in his own defense.

It was so much easier when I was a Lone Dog. A Lone Dog answers to nobody. But what if I'm not meant to be a Lone Dog at all?

Lucky swallowed, his throat dry. "It is true that I have been helping both Packs," he began. A growl rose from the lean brown-and-white hunt-dog, Dart, and was quickly echoed by the long-eared littermates, Twitch and Spring. They had been his Packmates, but now they were glaring at him fiercely, their hackles raised. Lucky struggled not to turn and run into the forest. If he did that he could never, ever come back. He had to keep his courage.

"I have gotten to know you all," he said. "And I've been thinking . . . what if my original mission to join the Wild Pack was *meant to be*? The Earth-Dog growled; the River-Dog revealed the path of fresh water; the Forest-Dog protected me on the way to this camp. At each turn I met friends . . . Sweet in the Trap House. My litter-sister Bella . . . even the Sky and Moon Dogs seem to have led me to this point."

Dart still growled, but the others grew quiet. Lucky could tell that he had their attention.

"See how the Packs joined to fight the foxes?" he went on. "Everyone had a role—not just big dogs like Fiery and Martha, but smaller fighters like Snap and Daisy. Dogs from different backgrounds, wild and leashed . . ." He paused, his eyes trailing over the assembled dogs. "You don't even know one another, yet you all fought fearlessly for a single purpose. Maybe the Spirit Dogs brought me here so that both Packs could unite?"

Alpha's face contorted in a menacing snarl but Snap, the Wild Pack's white-and-tan hunter, had a thoughtful look on her face. A few paces away, Moon and Fiery were still standing by their remaining pups. They exchanged glances and Moon stepped forward.

"Without the Leashed Dogs' help, we would have lost all three of our pups, not just little Fuzz."

Alpha watched her a moment and turned back to Lucky. The dog-wolf's yellow eyes bore into him. "That does not change the fact that he deceived us," he snarled. "Lucky brought danger and death into our camp." He turned his fierce gaze on the Leashed Dogs. "My Pack had to save this band of weaklings many times during the battle with the foxes. We cannot be expected to protect grown dogs who are feeble as pups."

Daisy bristled at this insult and Mickey scratched the grass next to his longpaw's glove with a forepaw.

But it was Bella who stepped forward.

Lucky's heart tightened in his chest. If his litter-sister challenged Alpha, she'd only make matters worse. He might destroy Lucky and throw out the Leashed Dogs just to teach her a lesson. But Bella dipped her head, addressing Alpha respectfully without looking up.

"I am sorry that I brought the foxes to your camp. It was unwise, and it was *stupid* of me." Her tail fell limp behind her. "I was duped into believing that foxes would act honorably. It was a mistake I will never make again. Truthfully, we wanted only to *share* in what you have here. We didn't intend to harm your Pack."

Alpha growled at this, his ears erect and his upper lip peeling back to reveal his fangs.

Lucky watched in astonishment as Bella lowered herself onto the ground submissively. With a whine she rolled to expose her belly. "I make you a solemn promise, Alpha, on behalf of my Pack. If you let us stay, the Leashed Dogs will serve you faithfully. We will obey your commands and fight alongside you, making your Pack even more formidable. We are better hunters than we look and we are keen to help with the tasks of the Pack. All we ask is to share in your food and water, and that you spare Lucky. He meant you no harm. He didn't know our plans; I swear it. And he did his very best to defend the pups when the foxes attacked;

the Mother-Dog said so." Bella looked briefly at Moon, then lowered her muzzle.

Moon whined her agreement. Guarding the two remaining pups, Fiery licked their heads as they leaned against his forelegs.

Lucky's heart swelled in his ribs, his anger draining away. He knew what it had cost Bella to surrender to Alpha in front of both Packs. He was sure that the last thing she wanted was to serve the ruthless half wolf. She was doing it to provide for her Pack—and to save Lucky's skin.

She hasn't deserted me.

He remembered her as a puppy, when she was still known as Squeak, bright, bossy, curious, and loyal—she had always been loyal.

Alpha shook his shaggy gray fur and scratched a large, pointed ear with a ragged claw. He was looking around at his Pack, gauging their reaction to Bella's submissive speech. Dart's hackles were still raised, but Twitch and Spring seemed more relaxed, and Snap's tongue was lolling from her jaws in a grin. Whine turned away while Moon and Fiery stood tall and gazed back at their leader.

Lucky held his breath, waiting for Alpha's verdict.

"I am willing to let you join us," the dog-wolf said at last, "but you will take low positions. You will be trained as Patrol Dogs and given the most tiring routines. If you believe you are capable of joining the more prestigious hunting group, you will have to *earn* that right through hard work and honorable combat. Those are the rules of my Pack."

Martha, Bruno, and Daisy turned instinctively to Lucky, used to following his advice. Lucky licked his chops. What choice did they have? Without Alpha's permission, they would not have access to food or clean water, which was in the Wild Pack's territory.

Before he could say anything, Alpha spoke again. "Foolish Leashed Dogs, looking to him. Don't you know that he's the lowest-ranking member of your new Pack? The *Omega*."

Alpha glared at the Leashed Dogs, challenging them to respond, but none of them dared. Lucky saw Whine smirk, his ugly face a crisscross of wrinkles. Lucky lowered his head, biting back a snarl. He remembered all too well the humiliations that Whine had faced as the lowliest Pack member.

But Alpha wasn't finished yet. "And the new Omega will be given a permanent reminder of his treachery: a scar on his flank so that none can forget what he has done."

Lucky yelped. He thought of Mulch, who'd been blamed for

eating out of turn . . . framed by Lucky and Whine, to get him demoted to Omega. Alpha had sprung at Mulch, scraping and gouging. Sweet had backed him up, adding savage bites to Mulch's wounds.

"Oh, Alpha," whined Martha, the huge Leashed Dog with webbed paws. "Be merciful!"

By her side, little Daisy yipped: "Please. Lucky will do everything you say; we promise. You don't have to do this."

Lucky whined softly with gratitude as Twitch and Spring joined the chorus of protests. "We agree," barked Twitch. "Becoming Omega is enough punishment."

Fiery cocked his head questioningly and even Sweet seemed unsure, though she stayed silent.

Alpha howled to be heard, his wolfish cry cutting through the whines and yaps. "The Pack will need stricter rules if it's to survive with all these extra dogs! That will be the price of Lucky treachery and deceit."

Lucky couldn't imagine any stricter rules—Alpha's Pack already so organized, the hunting and eating rights clea mented. A dog's rank even dictated where he slept!

Lucky had risked his life to battle the foxes, and y Pack's leader was determined to hurt and humiliate throbbed and his head felt thick and heavy, a grim reminder of that furious tussle.

The dogs were growling, barking, arguing with one another—divided over Lucky's fate.

"Wait!" snapped Mickey, the Farm Dog. He stood over his longpaw's glove, his ears flat but his head held high. "We're wasting time fighting with one another. We should be devoting our energies to surviving in this strange world, not arguing about who is higher in the Pack." Mickey tapped the glove absently with his paw. "Bella and Daisy are good hunters. The Pack would benefit from their skills. Why *wait* to use them?"

"Because we must have order," said Snap, the white-and-tan ⸱rel from the Wild Pack. "It's not about whether you *like* it—a ⸱t work without order. That's how it's always been." She ⸱ably, without anger or malice.

⸱s pricked up. "The Big Growl changed all the ⸱ are joining Packs, and Pack Dogs need to ⸱oesn't seem necessary—not anymore. It ⸱d."

⸱ey say so much.

⸱hough considering his words.

⸱in, Alpha sprang toward Mickey.

9

eating out of turn . . . framed by Lucky and Whine, to get him demoted to Omega. Alpha had sprung at Mulch, scraping and gouging. Sweet had backed him up, adding savage bites to Mulch's wounds.

"Oh, Alpha," whined Martha, the huge Leashed Dog with webbed paws. "Be merciful!"

By her side, little Daisy yipped: "Please. Lucky will do everything you say; we promise. You don't have to do this."

Lucky whined softly with gratitude as Twitch and Spring joined the chorus of protests. "We agree," barked Twitch. "Becoming Omega is enough punishment."

Fiery cocked his head questioningly and even Sweet seemed unsure, though she stayed silent.

Alpha howled to be heard, his wolfish cry cutting through the whines and yaps. "The Pack will need stricter rules if it's to survive with all these extra dogs! That will be the price of Lucky's treachery and deceit."

Lucky couldn't imagine any stricter rules—Alpha's Pack was already so organized, the hunting and eating rights clearly regimented. A dog's rank even dictated where he slept!

Lucky had risked his life to battle the foxes, and yet the Wild Pack's leader was determined to hurt and humiliate him. His leg throbbed and his head felt thick and heavy, a grim reminder of that furious tussle.

The dogs were growling, barking, arguing with one another—divided over Lucky's fate.

"Wait!" snapped Mickey, the Farm Dog. He stood over his longpaw's glove, his ears flat but his head held high. "We're wasting time fighting with one another. We should be devoting our energies to surviving in this strange world, not arguing about who is higher in the Pack." Mickey tapped the glove absently with his paw. "Bella and Daisy are good hunters. The Pack would benefit from their skills. Why *wait* to use them?"

"Because we must have order," said Snap, the white-and-tan mongrel from the Wild Pack. "It's not about whether you *like* it—a Pack can't work without order. That's how it's always been." She spoke reasonably, without anger or malice.

Mickey's ears pricked up. "The Big Growl changed all the rules. Leashed Dogs are joining Packs, and Pack Dogs need to change too. Hierarchy doesn't seem necessary—not anymore. It just makes things complicated."

Lucky had rarely heard Mickey say so much.

Snap watched the Farm Dog, as though considering his words. But before she could speak again, Alpha sprang toward Mickey.

Standing over the cowering black-and-white dog, he snarled: "The Big Growl is an even greater reason to *stick* to order and tradition. The world is more dangerous than ever. What we need is discipline, not some lazy group of ill-trained house-pets." He lifted his muzzle, his yellow eyes cold.

Most of the dogs lowered their heads, careful not to challenge the half wolf. None of them spoke.

Alpha looked from each dog to the next, then glared at Lucky. "It's time for the marking ceremony. Hold him down."

Panic surged through Lucky's body, his legs trembling and his paw pads growing damp with sweat. His eyes shot across the dogs, wondering who would launch the attack. Several of the Leashed Dogs whimpered, but they didn't dare speak up for him anymore. Even Bella, who had risen to her paws, said nothing.

Sweet broke forward. Lucky yelped in dismay as she pounced at his back, hugging his shoulders with her paws and bringing him down. His shoulder smacked the earth and a twinge shot through his injured leg. His body crackled with fear and panic. Sweet was stronger than she had been when they had escaped the Trap House. Snap leaped forward to assist Sweet, slamming into Lucky and helping to keep him pinned down. Lucky whimpered as Sweet's teeth sank into his neck.

"Relax," she whined as he kicked and twisted beneath her. "It will be easier for you if you don't struggle."

Lucky's heart thumped faster in his chest but for a moment he froze, seized by panic and confusion. Out of the corner of his eye, he saw the Leashed Dogs cringe. Sunshine started barking in her shrill yap. Martha looked away with an unhappy whine.

Bella found her voice again. "Please let him go; this isn't fair! What is the point of injuring him so badly that he can't hunt or shield us from attack? What good will that do any dog?"

Alpha growled impatiently. "None of an Omega's duties are so honorable. I won't cause him any serious injury." His lip curled as he approached Lucky, who started to thrash again, fighting against Sweet and Snap. "Just a good bite. Something he will never forget."

The surrounding dogs were barking wildly, scared and excited, as Alpha stepped forward. He loomed over Lucky.

Alpha snarled. "Be brave, traitor. It's time to take what's coming to you." His yellow eyes glittered and he licked his chops.

No! I won't let you do it! thought Lucky with a surge of anger. *You will not touch me!*

He shook and scrambled against Sweet until she loosened her hold on his neck; then he growled as he threw his forepaws against her. Sweet fell back, stunned, and Lucky spun his whole body around, forcing Snap off his back. He scrambled to his paws and pushed through the circle of dogs.

He threw a breathless look over his shoulder. The dog-wolf wasn't prepared for this. Alpha barked in fury as Lucky passed Bella and Daisy, who made no move to stop him. Sweet looked surprised, even upset.

I'm sorry, Sweet. I just can't stay here!

Lucky hesitated long enough for Snap to launch a second attack. He was about to throw her off when a great weight fell on top of him. Thick brown fur with black patches obscured his vision for a moment, and then he looked up into the pointed face of Bruno. His heavy, powerful body pressed Lucky to the ground and Lucky yelped, more from shock than pain.

Bruno! But he's a Leashed Dog!

Lucky could hardly believe it. A moment later Sweet had joined him, her forepaws digging into Lucky's neck. With three dogs holding him down, there was no way he could flee.

The dogs surrounding Lucky were barking feverishly. Sunshine, the white long-haired dog, hopped and spun in panicked circles while Mickey retreated a few paces, his longpaw glove held protectively between his teeth.

Alpha's shadow fell over Lucky as he drew closer, baring his gleaming fangs.

"A traitor walks among us," Alpha began. "According to tradition, he must be marked so that all may know what he has done. As Alpha, it is my duty to make this mark."

Lucky closed his eyes. He promised himself that, however badly it hurt, he would never let them know it. He would not whine, yelp, or howl as Alpha's teeth sank into his flank—he would not give Alpha the satisfaction.

Alpha brought his face to Lucky's ear and snarled softly. "You can forget your life of freedom now. You will be known as a traitor for as long as you live. No Pack will ever make the mistake of trusting you again."

The half wolf dipped his head, about to bury his fangs into Lucky's fur and flesh.

There was a high-pitched sound like shattering clear-stone. The air felt cold.

Alpha froze. The sound grew in volume, almost unbearably sharp. It clawed into Lucky's mind and chilled his blood. Pressed against him, he could feel Sweet's heart pounding and hear Snap whimpering with fear. Even Bruno gave a yelp of confusion.

Lucky's eyes rolled up to the sky. Squinting, he saw only the pale blue of sunup. Then another sound roared through the air. It was coming from the direction of the city, sounding like thunder—but longer, lower, and more menacing. Waves of anxious yaps ripped through the group of dogs.

"A storm!" barked Sweet, her heart racing as she pressed closer to Lucky.

More high-pitched shattering sent tremors through Lucky's whiskers. It sounded as though the sky were about to fall right on top of them! A moment later the air howled so shrill and loud, it drowned out even the wildest barks.

Lucky was dizzy with terror, his stomach clenching and his flanks heaving. The sky was sick, whining desperately like a dog in pain. This was no ordinary storm.

The howling air had *nothing* to do with the Sky-Dogs.

DON'T MISS
DAWN OF THE CLANS

WARRIORS

BOOK 1:
THE SUN TRAIL

For many moons, a tribe of cats has lived peacefully near the top of a mountain. But prey is scarce and seasons are harsh—and their leader fears they will not survive. When a mysterious vision reveals a land filled with food and water, a group of brave young cats sets off in search of a better home. But the challenges they face threaten to divide them, and the young cats must find a way to live side by side in peace.

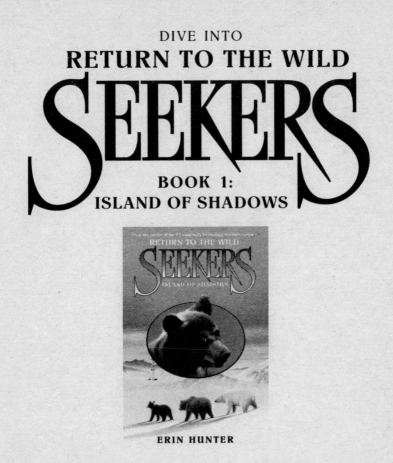
Toklo, Kallik, and Lusa survived the perilous mission that brought them together. Now, after their long, harrowing journey, the bears are eager to find the way home and share everything they've learned with the rest of their kinds. But the path that they travel is treacherous, and the strangers they meet could jeopardize everything the Seekers have fought for.

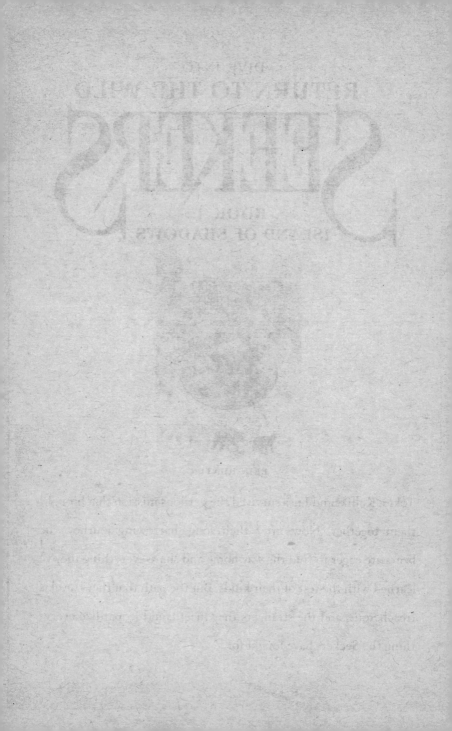

Warriors: The New Prophecy

Follow the next generation of heroic cats as they set off
on a quest to save the Clans from destruction.

Warriors: Power of Three

Firestar's grandchildren begin their training as warrior cats.
Prophecy foretells that they will hold more power than any cats before them.

Warriors: Omen of the Stars

Which ThunderClan apprentice will complete the prophecy that
foretells that three Clanmates hold the future of the Clans in their paws?